A COURT FOR THIEVES

(A THRONE FOR SISTERS -- BOOK 2)

MORGAN RICE

iSBN: 978-1-64029-176-8

Books by Morgan Rice

THE WAY OF STEEL
ONLY THE WORTHY (Book #1)

A THRONE FOR SISTERS
A THRONE FOR SISTERS (Book #1)
A COURT FOR THIEVES (Book #2)
A SLONG FOR ORPHANS (Book #3)

OF CROWNS AND GLORY
SLAVE, WARRIOR, QUEEN (Book #1)
ROGUE, PRISONER, PRINCESS (Book #2)
KNIGHT, HEIR, PRINCE (Book #3)
REBEL, PAWN, KING (Book #4)
SOLDIER, BROTHER, SORCERER (Book #5)
HERO, TRAITOR, DAUGHTER (Book #6)
RULER, RIVAL, EXILE (Book #7)
VICTOR, VANQUISHED, SON (Book #8)

KINGS AND SORCERERS
RISE OF THE DRAGONS (Book #1)
RISE OF THE VALIANT (Book #2)
THE WEIGHT OF HONOR (Book #3)
A FORGE OF VALOR (Book #4)
A REALM OF SHADOWS (Book #5)
NIGHT OF THE BOLD (Book #6)

THE SORCERER'S RING
A QUEST OF HEROES (Book #1)
A MARCH OF KINGS (Book #2)
A FATE OF DRAGONS (Book #3)
A CRY OF HONOR (Book #4)
A VOW OF GLORY (Book #5)
A CHARGE OF VALOR (Book #6)
A RITE OF SWORDS (Book #7)
A GRANT OF ARMS (Book #8)
A SKY OF SPELLS (Book #9)
A SEA OF SHIELDS (Book #10)

CHAPTER ONE

They made a spectacle of Sophia's punishment, as Sophia should have known they would. They dragged her back to the House of the Unclaimed, only pulling the hood from her head once they reached its confines, shoving her along with stumbling steps through the streets of Ashton.

Kate, help me! Sophia sent, knowing that her sister was her best option of getting through this.

Nobody helped her, not even those she passed by. They knew she wasn't some rich girl being kidnapped, just one of the indentured being taken back to face justice. Even hooded and wearing the rich dress of her disguise, it seemed that people could see that much. She could see their thoughts, with so many of them thinking she deserved it that she felt as though she were being spit on as they dragged her.

The masked nuns rang bells when her captors dragged her back. It might have seemed like a celebration, but Sophia knew it for what it was: a summons. They were dragging children from their beds to see what became of the ones who were stupid enough to run.

Sophia could see them now, clustered around the doorways and the windows of the orphanage. There were the older ones she knew, and younger ones who had only just come into what passed for the care of the place. All of them would watch what happened to her, and probably some of them would have nightmares about it afterward. The masked nuns wanted the children there to remember what they were, and to learn that there could be nothing better for them.

"Help me!" she called to them, but it made no difference.

She could see their thoughts. Some were too scared to move, some were still blinking with no understanding of what was happening. A few even thought that she deserved this; that she ought to be punished for breaking the rules.

The nuns pulled Sophia's outer dress from her. Sophia tried to struggle, but one of the nuns just slapped her for it while the others held her in place.

1

"Do you think you get to wear finery? A shameless thing like you deserves no rich clothes. You barely deserve the life the goddess chose to give you."

They stripped her down to her plain underdress, ignoring Sophia's shame at it. They ripped the braids of her hair into wildness, not allowing her even that much control over how she looked. Whenever she gave them the slightest resistance, they hit her with open hands, leaving her reeling from it. Still, they marched her forward.

Sister O'Venn was one of the most eager to do it. She marched Sophia forward, speaking all the time at a volume the watching inhabitants of the orphanage were sure to hear.

"Did you think that you would be out in the world for long?" she demanded. "The Masked Goddess demands that her debts are paid! Did you think that a shameless thing like you could avoid it just by giving herself to some rich man?"

Was that a guess, or did they somehow know what Sophia had been doing? If so, how could they?

"Look at her," Sister O'Venn called to the watching children. "Look at what happens to the ingrates and the runaways. The Masked Goddess gives you shelter here, asking only work in return! She gives you the chance of lives filled with meaning. Reject that and this is the price!"

Sophia could feel the fear of the orphans around her, so many thoughts together forming a wave of it. A few debated helping her, but there was never any real chance of it. Most were simply grateful that it wasn't them.

Sophia fought as they dragged her to the courtyard, but it made no difference. Perhaps Kate could have battled her way clear of them, but Sophia had never been a fighter. She'd been the clever one, only she hadn't been clever enough. She'd been caught, and now...

...now there was a post awaiting her at the center of the courtyard, its intention obvious.

There were jeers from some of the children there as the nuns led Sophia to that post, and that hurt almost more than the rest of it. She knew why they were doing it, because if she'd been up there she would have joined in, if only to ensure that she wouldn't be singled out for some punishment. Even so, Sophia felt tears in her eyes as she looked around at the anger in some of the young faces watching.

She was going to be a warning to them. For the rest of their lives, they would think about her anytime they thought about escaping.

Sophia called out with her powers as they tied her to the post, pressing her face to it and holding her in place with ropes of rough hemp.

Kate, help! They caught me!

There was no answer, though, as the nuns continued to tie Sophia in place like some sacrifice to the darker things people had worshipped before the Masked Goddess. She screamed for help with all the mental effort she could summon, but it didn't seem to make any difference.

The nuns took their time. This was obviously intended to be about theater as much as pain. Or maybe they just didn't want Sophia able to give with any of the blows that followed to reduce their sting.

Once Sophia was tied in place, the nuns led some of the younger children in, making them look at her as though she were some wild beast caught in a menagerie.

"We must be grateful," Sister O'Venn said. "We must be humble. We must repay the Masked Goddess what we owe her for her gifts. Fail, and there is a price. This girl ran. This girl was arrogant enough to set herself above the goddess's will. This girl was wanton and proud."

She said it like a judge passing sentence, even before she moved close to Sophia. It was starting to rain now, and Sophia could feel the cold of it in the dark.

"Repent," she said. "Repent your sins, and pay the goddess the price for your forgiveness!"

She'll suffer either way, but she must choose.

Sophia could see the same sentiment in the thoughts of the others. They meant to hurt her just as much regardless of what she said. There was no point in trying to lie and beg forgiveness, because the truth was that even the meekest of the sisters there wanted to hurt her. They wanted to do it as an example to the others, because they genuinely believed that it would be good for her soul, or simply because they liked watching people hurt. Sister O'Venn was one of the latter.

"I'm sorry," Sophia said. She could see the others there, drinking in her words. "I'm sorry I didn't run twice as fast! You should all run," she shouted to the children there. "They can't stop all of you. They can't *catch* all of you!"

3

Sister O'Venn slapped her head against the wood of the punishment post, then shoved a length of dowel between Sophia's teeth so roughly it was a miracle she didn't snap any.

"So that you don't bite your tongue screaming," she said with a mock sweetness that had nothing to do with the things Sophia could see in her mind. Sophia could understand Kate's urge for revenge then, her wish to burn it down around them. She would have set light to Sister O'Venn without a second thought.

The masked sister brought out a whip, testing it where Sophia could see. It was an evil-looking thing, with multiple strands of leather, all with knots along their length. It was the kind of thing that could bruise and tear, far harsher than any of the belts or rods that had been used to beat Sophia in the past. She tried to struggle clear of her bonds, but it made no difference. The best she could hope for was to stand there defiantly as they punished her.

When Sister O'Venn struck her for the first time, Sophia almost bit through the wooden dowel. Agony exploded through her back, and she could feel it tearing open under the blows.

Please, Kate she sent, *please!*

Again, there was the sensation of her words floating off without connection, without answer. Had her sister heard them? It was impossible to know, when there was no reply. Sophia could only hang there, and hope, and call for her.

Sophia tried not to scream at first, if only to deny Sister O'Venn what she really wanted, but the truth was that there was no holding it at bay when pain like fire burned across her back. Sophia screamed with every impact, until it felt as though there was nothing left within her.

When they finally pulled the dowel from her mouth, Sophia tasted blood on it.

"Do you repent now, you evil girl?" the masked sister demanded.

Sophia would have killed her if there had been even a moment's opportunity, would have run a thousand times if she thought that there was a chance she could get away. Even so, she forced her sobbing body to nod, hoping that she could look contrite enough.

"Please," she begged. "I'm sorry. I shouldn't have run."

Sister O'Venn leaned in close enough to laugh at her then. Sophia could see the anger there, and the hunger for more.

"Do you think I can't tell when a girl is lying?" she demanded. "I should have known from the moment you came here that you were a wicked thing, given where you came from. I'll make you properly penitent, though. I'll beat the wickedness out of you if I have to!"

She turned to the others there, and Sophia hated the fact that they were still just watching, still as statues, frightened into immobility. Why weren't they helping her? Why weren't they at least recoiling in horror, running from the House of the Unclaimed to get as far away from the things it did as they could? They all just stood there while Sister O'Venn stalked in front of them, her bloodied scourge hanging in her hand.

"You come to us as nothing, as evidence of another's sin, or as drains upon the world!" the masked nun called. "You leave here shaped into boys and girls ready to serve the world as you are required. This one sought to run before her indenture. She took years of safety and instruction here, and she tried to run from what it costs!"

Because what it cost was the rest of the orphans' lives, spent indentured to whoever could afford the cost of their upbringing. They might theoretically be able to repay the cost, but how many did that, and what did they suffer in the years it took them?

"This one should have been indentured days ago!" the masked nun said, pointing. "Well, tomorrow, she will be. She will be sold as the ungrateful wretch that she is, and there will be no easy time for her now. There will be no kind men looking for a bought wife, or nobles looking for a servant."

That was what passed for a fine life, an easy life, in this place. Sophia hated that fact almost as much as she hated the people there. She hated the thought of what might happen to her too. She'd been about to become the wife of a prince, and now…

"The only ones who will want a wicked thing like this," Sister O'Venn said, "are cruel men with crueler aims. This girl brought it upon herself, and now she will go where she must."

"Where you choose to send me!" Sophia countered, because she could see from the masked nun's thoughts that she had sent for the worst people she could think of. There was a kind of torment just in being able to see that. She looked around again at each of the masked nuns there, trying to stare through the veils to reach the women beneath.

"I'm only going to people like that because you choose to send me. You *choose* to indenture us. You sell us as though we're nothing!"

"You are nothing," Sister O'Venn said, shoving the dowel back into Sophia's mouth.

Sophia glared at her, reaching out to try to find some speck of humanity somewhere in there. There was nothing that she could find, only cruelty masquerading as necessary firmness, and evil pretending to be duty, without even real belief behind it. Sister O'Venn just liked to hurt the weak.

She hurt Sophia then, and there was nothing Sophia could do except scream.

She threw herself against the ropes, trying to tear free, or at least find some iota of room in which to escape the scourge ripping out penitence from her. There was nothing she could do, though, except scream, begging mutely into the wood she bit into while her power sent her screams out into the city, hoping that her sister would hear them somewhere in Ashton.

There was no reply except the steady whistle of braided leather through the air and the slap of it against her bloodied back. The masked nun beat her with a seemingly interminable strength, long past the point where Sophia's legs could hold her up, and past the point where she even had the strength left to scream.

At some point after that, she must have passed out, but that made no difference. By that point, even Sophia's nightmares were things of violence, bringing back old dreams of a burning house and men she had to outrun. When she came back to herself, they were done, the others long gone.

Still tied in place, Sophia wept while the rain washed away the blood of her beating. It would have been easy to believe that it couldn't get worse, except that it could.

It could get so much worse.

And tomorrow, it would.

CHAPTER TWO

Kate stood above Ashton and watched it burn. She had thought that she would be happy to see it gone, but this wasn't just the House of the Unclaimed or the spaces where the dock workers kept their barges.

This was everything.

Wood and thatch caught light, and Kate could feel the terror of the people there within the wide circle of houses. Cannon roared over the screams of the dying, and Kate saw swathes of buildings falling as easily as if they were made from paper. Blunderbusses sounded, while arrows filled the air so thickly it was hard to see the sky beyond them. They fell, and Kate walked through the rain of them with the strange, detached calm that could only come from being in a dream.

No, not a dream. This was more than that.

Whatever the powers of Siobhan's fountain, they ran through Kate now, and she saw death all around her. Horses ran through the streets, riders cutting downward with sabers and backswords. Screams came from all around her until they seemed to fill the city as surely as the fire did. Even the river appeared to be on fire now, although as Kate looked, she saw that it was the barges that filled the broad expanse of it, fire leaping from one to another as men fought to get clear. Kate had been on a barge, and she could guess at how terrifying those flames must be.

There were figures running through the streets, and it was easy to tell the difference between the panicked citizens of the city and the figures in ochre-colored uniforms who followed with blades, hacking at them as they ran. Kate had never seen the sack of a city before, but this was something awful. It was violence for the sake of it, with no sign of stopping.

There were lines of refugees beyond the city now, heading out with whatever possessions they could carry in long rows heading out into the rest of the country. Would they seek refuge in the Ridings or go further, out to towns like Treford or Barriston?

Then Kate saw the riders bearing down on them, and she knew that they wouldn't make it that far. There was fire at the back of them, though, so there was nowhere to run. What would it be like to be caught like that?

She knew, though, didn't she?

The scene shifted, and now Kate knew that she wasn't looking at something that might be, but something that *had* been. She knew this dream, because it was one that she had far too often. She was in an old house, a grand house, and there was danger coming.

There was something different this time though. There were people there, and Kate looked up at them from so far below that she knew she must have been tiny. There was a man there, looking worried but strong in a nobleman's velvet, hastily thrown on, and a curled black wig discarded in his rush to deal with the situation, revealing cropped gray hair below. The woman with him was lovely but disheveled, as if it normally took her an hour to dress with the aid of servants and now she'd done it in minutes. She had a kind look to her, and Kate reached out to her, not understanding why the woman didn't pick her up, when that was what she usually did.

"There's no time," the man said. "And if we all try to break free, they will just follow. We need to go separately."

"But the children—" the woman began. Kate knew now without being told that this was her mother.

"They will be safer away from us," her father said. He turned to a servant, and Kate recognized her nurse. "You need to get them out, Anora. Take them somewhere safe, where no one will know them. We will find them when this madness is done."

Kate saw Sophia then, looking far too young, but also looking ready to argue. Kate knew that look far too well.

"No," their mother said. "You have to go, both of you. There is no time. Run, my darlings." There was a crash from somewhere else in the house. "*Run.*"

Kate was running then, her hand held firmly in Sophia's. There was a crash, but she didn't look back. She just kept going, out along corridors, pausing only to hide as shadowy figures passed. They ran until they found an open set of windows, heading out of the house, out into the darkness…

Kate blinked, coming back to herself. The morning light above her seemed too bright, the shine of it dazzling. She tried to grab for the dream as she woke, tried to see what had happened next, but it was already fleeing faster than she could hold to it. Kate groaned at that, because she knew that the last part hadn't been a dream. It had been a memory, and it was one memory that Kate wanted to be able to see more than all the others.

Still, she had her parents' faces in her mind now. She held them there, forcing herself not to forget. She sat up slowly, her head swimming with the aftermath of what she'd seen.

"You should take it slowly," Siobhan said. "The fountain's waters can have aftereffects."

She was sitting on the edge of the fountain, which looked ruined again now, not bright and fresh as it had been when Siobhan had drawn water from it for Kate to drink. She looked exactly the same as she had what must have been a night ago, even the flowers twined into her hair looking untouched, as though she hadn't moved in all that time. She was watching Kate with an expression that said nothing about what she was thinking, and the walls that she kept around her mind meant that she was a total blank, even to Kate's power.

Kate tried to stand simply because she wouldn't be stopped from it by this woman. The forest around her seemed to swim as she did, and Kate saw a haze of colors around the edges of trees, stones, branches. Kate stumbled, having to rest her hand against a broken column to steady herself.

"You will have to learn to listen to me if you're to be my apprentice," Siobhan said. "You can't expect to be able to simply stand up after that many changes in your body."

Kate gritted her teeth and waited for the sensation of dizziness to pass. It didn't take long. Judging by her expression, even Siobhan was surprised when Kate stepped away from the support of the column.

"Not bad," she said. "You're adjusting quicker than I might have thought. How do you feel?"

Kate shook her head. "I don't know."

"Then take the time to think," Siobhan snapped back with just a hint of annoyance. "I want a student who thinks about the world, rather than just reacting to it. I think that's you. Do you want to prove me wrong?"

Kate shook her head again. "I'm getting… the world seems different when I look at it."

"You're starting to see it as it is, with the currents of life," Siobhan said. "You will get used to it. Try moving."

Kate took a faltering step, then another.

"You can do better than that," Siobhan said. "Run!"

That was a little too close to Kate's dreams for comfort, and she found herself wondering how much of it Siobhan had seen. She had said that she and Kate weren't the same, but if they were close

9

enough for the other woman to want to teach her, then maybe they were close enough for Siobhan to see into her dreams.

There was no time to think about that right then, because Kate was too busy running. She sprinted through the woods, her feet skimming over the moss and the mud, the fallen leaves and the broken branches. It was only as she saw the trees whipping by that she realized just how fast she was moving.

Kate leapt, and suddenly she was springing into the lower branches of one of the trees around her, as easily as if she'd stepped up from a boat to a dock. Kate balanced on the branch, seeming to feel every breath of wind that moved it before it could shake her off. She hopped back down to the ground and, on impulse, moved to a heavy fallen branch that she could never have hoped to lift before. Kate felt the roughness of the bark against her hands as she gripped it, and she lifted it smoothly, hoisting it above her head like one of the strongmen at the fairs that came to Ashton every so often. She threw it, watching the branch disappear into the trees to land with a crash.

Kate heard it, and for a moment, she heard every other sound around her in the forest. She heard the rustle of leaves as small things moved under them, the chirp of birds up in the branches. She heard the scuff of tiny feet against the ground, and knew the spot where a hare would appear before it came. The sheer panoply of sounds was too much at first. Kate had to clamp her hands to her ears to keep out the drip of water from leaves, the movement of insects along bark. She clamped down on it the way she'd learned to with her talent for hearing thoughts.

She returned to the spot where the ruined fountain stood, and Siobhan was there, smiling with what seemed to be a hint of pride.

"What is happening to me?" Kate asked.

"Only what you asked for," Siobhan said. "You wanted strength to defeat your enemies."

"But all of this…" Kate began. The truth was that she'd never believed so much could happen to her.

"There are many forms that magic can take," Siobhan said. "You will not curse your enemies or scry on them from a distance. You will not call down lightning or summon the spirits of the restless dead. Those are paths for others."

Kate raised an eyebrow. "Is any of that even possible?"

She saw Siobhan shrug. "It doesn't matter. You have the strength of the fountain running in you now. You will be faster and stronger, your senses will be sharper. You will see things that most people cannot. Combined with your own talents, you will be formidable. I will teach you to strike in battle or from the shadows. I will make you deadly."

Kate had always wanted to be strong, but even so, she found herself a little scared by it all. Siobhan had already told her that there would be a price for all of this, and the more wonderful it seemed, the greater she suspected that price was going to be. She thought back to what she'd dreamed, and she hoped that it wasn't a warning.

"I saw something," Kate said. "I dreamed it, but it didn't feel like a dream."

"What did it feel like?" Siobhan asked.

Kate was about to say that she didn't know, but she caught Siobhan's expression and thought better of it. "It felt like the truth. I hope not, though. In my dream, Ashton was in the middle of being razed. It was on fire, and the people were being slaughtered."

She half expected Siobhan to laugh at her for even mentioning it, or maybe she hoped for it. Instead, Siobhan looked thoughtful, nodding to herself.

"I should have expected it," the woman said. "Things are moving faster than I thought they would, but time is one thing even I cannot do anything about. Well, not permanently."

"You know what's happening?" Kate asked.

That earned her a smile that she couldn't decipher. "Let's just say that I have been expecting events," Siobhan replied. "There are things that I have anticipated, and things that must be done in only a short amount of time."

"And you aren't going to tell me what's going on, are you?" Kate said. She tried to keep the frustration out of her voice by focusing on everything that she had gained. She was stronger now, and faster, so should it matter that she didn't know everything? It did though.

"Already, you're learning," Siobhan replied. "I knew I didn't make a mistake in choosing you for an apprentice."

In choosing her? Kate had been the one to seek out the fountain, not once, but twice. She'd been the one to ask for power, and the one to decide to accept Siobhan's terms. She wasn't going to let the other woman persuade her that it had been any other way.

"I came here," Kate said. "I chose this."

Siobhan shrugged. "Yes, you did. And now, it is time for you to begin to learn."

Kate looked around. This wasn't a library like the one in the city. It wasn't a training field with fencing masters like the one where Will's regiment had humiliated her. What could she learn, here in this wild place?

Even so, she prepared herself, standing in front of Siobhan and waiting. "I'm ready. What do I have to do?"

Siobhan cocked her head to one side. "Wait."

She went to a spot where a small fire had been laid in a pit, ready to light. Siobhan tossed a flicker of flame into it without bothering with a flint and steel, then whispered words Kate couldn't catch as smoke rose from it.

The smoke started to twist and writhe, forming itself into shapes as Siobhan directed it the way a conductor might have directed musicians. The smoke coalesced in a shape that was vaguely human, finally burning away to leave something that looked like a warrior from some long gone age. He stood holding a sword that looked wickedly sharp.

So sharp, in fact, that Kate had no time to even react when he thrust it through her heart.

CHAPTER THREE

They left Sophia to dangle in place for the night, held up only by the ropes they'd used to tie her to the punishment post. The sheer immobility of it was almost as much of a torture as her ravaged back, as her limbs burned with the lack of movement. She couldn't do anything to ease the pain of her beating, or the shame of being left out there in the rain as a kind of warning to the others there.

Sophia hated them then, with the kind of hatred she had always chided Kate for holding too close. She wanted to watch them die, and the wanting of it was a kind of pain too, because there was no way that Sophia would ever be in a position to make it happen. She couldn't even free herself now.

She couldn't sleep either. The pain and the awkward position saw to that. The closest Sophia could come was a kind of half-dreaming delirium, the past mixing with the present while the rain continued to plaster her hair to her head.

She dreamed of the cruelty she'd seen in Ashton, and not just in the living hell of the orphanage. The streets had been almost as bad with their predators and their callous lack of care for those who ended up on them. Even in the palace, for every kindly soul, there had been another like Milady d'Angelica who seemed to revel in the power her position gave her to be cruel to others. She thought of a world that was filled with wars and human-wrought cruelty, wondering how it could have turned into such a heartless place.

Sophia tried to turn her thoughts to kinder things, but that wasn't easy. She started to think about Sebastian, but the truth was that it hurt too much. Things had seemed so perfect between them, and then, when he'd found out what she was... it had fallen apart so quickly that now Sophia's heart felt like ash. He hadn't even tried to stand up to his mother or to stay with Sophia. He'd just sent her away.

Sophia thought about Kate instead, and thoughts of her brought with them the need to cry for help once more. She sent another call into the first glimmers of the dawn light, but still, there was nothing. Worse, thinking about her sister mostly brought with it memories of hard times in the orphanage, or other, earlier things.

Sophia thought about the fire. The attack. She'd been so young when it had happened that she barely remembered any of it. She could recall her mother's and father's faces, but not what they had sounded like outside of those few instructions to run. She could remember having to flee, but could only pull together the faintest glimpses of the time before that. There had been a wooden rocking horse, a large house where it had been easy to play at getting lost, a nanny...

Sophia couldn't dredge up more than that from her memory. The House of the Unclaimed had covered it almost completely with a miasma made from pain, so that it was hard to think past the beatings and the grinding wheels, the enforced subservience and the dread that came from knowing what it all led to.

The same thing that awaited Sophia now: being sold like an animal.

How long did she hang there, held in place no matter how she tried to get away? Long enough that the sun was over the horizon, at least. Long enough that when the masked nuns came to cut her down, Sophia's limbs gave way, leaving her to collapse to the courtyard's stones. The nuns made no move to help her.

"Get up," one of them ordered. "You don't want your debt to be sold looking like that."

Sophia continued to lie there, gritting her teeth against the pain as feeling crept back into her legs. She only moved when the nun lashed out, kicking her.

"Get up, I said," she snapped.

Sophia forced herself to her feet, and the masked nuns took her by the arms the way Sophia imagined a prisoner might be escorted to her execution. She didn't feel much better at the prospect of what was due to come for her.

They took her to a small stone cell, where there were buckets waiting. They scrubbed her then, and somehow the masked nuns managed to turn even that into a kind of torture. Some of the water was so hot that it scalded Sophia's skin as it washed away the blood, making her scream with all the pain that she'd experienced when Sister O'Venn had beaten her.

More of the water was icy cold, in a way that made Sophia shiver with it. Even the soap the nuns used stung, burning at her eyes as they scrubbed her hair and bound it back in a rough knot that had nothing to do with the elegant designs of the palace. They took away her white underdress and gave her the gray shift of the orphanage to wear. After the fine clothes Sophia had worn in the previous days, it scratched at her skin with the promise of biting insects. They didn't feed her. Presumably, it wasn't worth it, now that their investment in her was at an end.

That was what this place was. It was like a farm for children, fattening them up just enough with skills and fear to make useful apprentices or servants and then selling them on.

"You know that this is wrong," Sophia said as they marched her toward the door. "Can't you see the things you're doing?"

Another of the nuns cuffed her at the back of the head, making Sophia stumble.

"We provide the Masked Goddess's mercy to those who need it. Now, be silent. You'll fetch a worse price if your face is bruised from being slapped."

Sophia swallowed at that thought. It hadn't occurred to her quite how carefully they'd hidden the marks of her beating beneath the dull gray of her shift. Again, she found herself thinking of farmers, although now it was about the kind of horse trader who might dye a horse's coat for a better sale.

They took her along the corridors of the orphanage, and now there were no watching faces. They didn't want the children there to see this part, probably because it would remind too many of them of the fate that was to come for them. It would encourage them to run, when the beating last night had probably terrified them into never daring it.

In any case, they were heading into the sections of the House of the Unclaimed where the children didn't go now, into the spaces reserved for the nuns and their visitors. Most of it was plain, although there were notes of wealth here and there, in gilded candlesticks, or in the shine of silver around a ceremonial mask's edges.

The room they led Sophia to was practically plush by the standards of the orphanage. It looked a little like the receiving parlor of some noble house, with chairs set around the edges, each with a small table holding a goblet of wine and a plate with sweetmeats. There was a table at one end of the room, behind which Sister O'Venn stood, a length of folded vellum beside her. Sophia guessed that it would be the tally for her indenture. Would they even let her know the amount before they sold it on?

"Formally," Sister O'Venn said, "we are required to ask you, before we sell on your indenture, if you have the means to repay your debt to the goddess. The amount is here. Come, you worthless thing, and find out what you're *actually* worth."

Sophia didn't get a choice; they took her to the table and she looked down at it. She wasn't surprised to find every meal, every night of lodging annotated. It came to so much that Sophia recoiled from it instinctively.

"Do you have the means to pay this debt?" the nun repeated.

Sophia stared up at her. "You know I don't."

There was a stool in the middle of the floor, carved from hard wood and completely at odds with the rest of the room. Sister O'Venn pointed to it.

"Then you will sit there, and do so demurely. You will not speak unless required to. You will obey any instruction instantly. Fail, and there will be punishment."

Sophia hurt too much to disobey. She went to the low stool and sat, keeping her eyes downcast enough that she wouldn't attract the attention of the nuns. Even so, she watched as figures came into the room, men and women, all with the sense of wealth around them. Sophia couldn't see much more of them than that, though, because they wore veils not unlike those of the nuns, obviously so no one would see who was interested in buying her like chattel.

"Thank you for coming in at such short notice," Sister O'Venn said, and now her voice held the smoothness of a merchant extolling the virtues of some fine silk or perfume. "I hope that you will find it worthwhile. Please take a moment to examine the girl, and then make your bids with me."

They surrounded Sophia then, staring at her the way a cook might have examined a cut of meat at the market, wondering what it would be good for, trying to see any trace of rot or excessive sinew. A woman ordered Sophia to look at her, and Sophia did her best to obey.

"Her coloring is good," the woman said, "and I suppose she might be pretty enough."

"A pity they won't let us see her with a boy," a fat man said with a trace of an accent that said he'd come from across the Knifewater. His expensive silks were stained with old sweat, the stink of it disguised by a perfume probably better suited to a woman. He glanced over to the nuns as if Sophia wasn't there. "Unless your opinion on that has changed, sisters?"

"This is still a place of the Goddess," Sister O'Venn said, and Sophia could pick out the genuine disapproval in her voice. Strange that she would balk at that, when she didn't at so much else, Sophia thought.

She reached out with her talent, trying to pick out what she could from the minds of those there. She didn't know what she hoped to accomplish, though, because there was no way she could think of to influence their opinions of her one way or another.

Instead, it just gave her an opportunity to see the same cruelties, the same harsh ends, again and again. The best she could hope for was servitude. The worst made her shiver with fear.

"Hmm, she does quiver beautifully when she's afraid," one man said. "Too fine for the mines, I guess, but I'll put in my bid."

He walked to Sister O'Venn, whispering a figure to her. One by one, the others did the same. When they were done, she looked around the room.

"Currently, Meister Karg has the highest bid," Sister O'Venn said. "Does anyone wish to raise their offer?"

A couple seemed to consider it. The woman who had wanted to look into Sophia's eyes walked over to the masked nun, presumably whispering another figure.

"Thank you, all of you," Sister O'Venn said at last. "Our business is concluded. Meister Karg, the contract of indenture now belongs to you. I am required to remind you that should it be repaid, this girl will be free to go."

The fat man snorted beneath his veil, pulling it away to reveal a ruddy face with too many chins and not improved by the presence of a bushy moustache.

"And when has that ever happened with my girls?" he shot back. He held out a pudgy hand. Sister O'Venn took the contract, placing it in his grip.

The others there made small sounds of irritation, although Sophia could sense that several of them were already thinking about other possibilities. The woman who had raised her bid was thinking that it was a pity she had lost, but only in the way it irritated her when one of her horses lost a race against those of her neighbors.

All the while, Sophia sat there, unable to move at the thought of having her entire life handed over to someone so easily. A few days ago, she'd been about to marry a prince, and now… now she was about to become this man's property?

"There is just the matter of the money," Sister O'Venn said.

The fat man, Meister Karg, nodded. "I will deal with it now. It is better to pay in coin than bankers' promises when there is a ship to catch."

A ship? What ship? Where did this man plan to take her? What was he going to do with her? The answers to that were easy enough to snatch from his thoughts, and just the idea of it was enough to make Sophia half rise, ready to run.

Strong hands caught her, the nuns clamping their grips around her arms once more. Meister Karg looked over at her with casual contempt.

"Have her taken to my wagon, would you? I will settle things here, and then…"

And then, Sophia could see that her life would become a thing of even worse horror. She wanted to fight, but there was nothing she could do as the others led her away. Nothing at all. In the privacy of her head, she screamed for her sister's help.

Yet it seemed that Kate either hadn't heard—or didn't care.

CHAPTER FOUR

Again and again, Kate died.

Or "died" at least. Illusory weapons slid into her flesh, ghostly hands strangled her into unconsciousness. Arrows flickered into existence and shot through her. The weapons were only things formed from smoke, pulled into existence by Siobhan's magic, but every one of them hurt as much as a real weapon would have.

They didn't kill Kate, though. Instead, each moment of pain merely brought a sound of disappointment from Siobhan, who watched from the sidelines with what seemed to be a combination of amusement and exasperation at the slowness with which Kate was learning.

"Pay attention, Kate," Siobhan said. "Do you think I'm summoning these dream fragments for my entertainment?"

The figure of a swordsman appeared in front of Kate, dressed for a duel rather than an all-out battle. He saluted her, leveling a rapier.

"This is the Finnochi derobement," he said in the same flat monotone the others seemed to have. He thrust at her and Kate went to parry with her wooden practice sword, because she'd learned to do that much, at least. She was fast enough to see the moment when the fragment changed direction, but the move still caught her off guard, the ephemeral blade slipping through her heart.

"Again," Siobhan said. "There is little time."

In spite of what she said, there seemed to be more time than Kate could have imagined. The minutes seemed to stretch out in the wood, filled with opponents trying to kill her, and as they tried, Kate learned.

She learned to fight them, cutting them down with her practice sword because Siobhan had insisted that she set her real blade aside to avoid the risk of real injury. She learned to thrust and cut, parry and feint, because every time she made a mistake, the ghostly outline of a blade slid into her with a pain that felt all too real.

After the ones with swords were the ones with sticks or mauls, bows or muskets. Kate learned to kill a dozen ways with her hands, and to read the moment when a foe would fire a weapon, throwing herself flat. She learned to run through the forest, jumping from branch to branch, fleeing from foes as she dodged and hid.

She learned to hide and move silently, because every time she made a noise, the ephemeral enemies descended on her with more weapons than she could match.

"Couldn't you just *teach* me?" Kate demanded of Siobhan, shouting it into the trees.

"I am teaching you," she replied as she stepped from one of those nearby. "If you were here to learn magic, we could do that with tomes and gentle words, but you are here to become deadly. For that, pain is the greatest teacher there is."

Kate gritted her teeth and kept going. At least here, there was a point to the pain, unlike in the House of the Unclaimed. She set off back into the forest, sticking to the shadows, learning to move without disturbing the least twig or leaf as she crept up on a fresh set of conjured foes.

Still she died.

Every time she succeeded, a new foe appeared, or a new threat. Each was harder than the last. When Kate learned to avoid human eyes, Siobhan conjured dogs whose skin seemed to billow into smoke with every step they took. When Kate learned to slip past the defenses of a duelist's sword, the next foe wore armor so that she could only strike at the gaps between the plates.

Whenever she stopped, it seemed that Siobhan was there, with advice or hints, encouragement or just the kind of maddening amusement that spurred Kate on to do better. She was faster now, and stronger, but it seemed as though it wasn't enough for the woman who controlled the fountain. She had the feeling that Siobhan was preparing her for something, but the other woman wouldn't say what, or answer any questions that weren't about what Kate needed to do next.

"You need to learn to use the talent that you were born with," Siobhan said. "Learn to see the intent of a foe before they strike. Learn to pick out the location of your enemies before they find you."

"How do I practice that when I'm fighting illusions?" Kate demanded.

"I direct them, so I will allow you to look at a fraction of my mind," Siobhan said. "Be careful though. There are places you do not want to look."

That caught Kate's interest. She'd already come up against the walls the other woman kept in place to stop her from looking at her mind. Now she was going to get to peek? When she felt Siobhan's walls shift, Kate plunged inside as far as the new boundaries would let her.

It wasn't far, but it was still far enough to get a sense of an alien mind, as far from any normal person's as Kate had ever seen. Kate recoiled from the sheer strangeness of it, pulling back. She did so just in time for an ephemeral foe to thrust a blade through her throat.

"I told you to be careful," Siobhan said while Kate gagged. "Now, try again."

There was another swordsman in front of Kate. She focused, and this time she caught the moment when Siobhan told it to attack. She ducked, cutting it down.

"Better," Siobhan said. It was as close to praise as she came, but praise didn't stop the constant testing. It just meant more foes, more work, more training. Siobhan pushed Kate until even with the new strength she had, she felt ready to collapse from exhaustion.

"Haven't I learned enough?" Kate asked. "Haven't I *done* enough?"

She watched Siobhan smile without amusement. "You think that you are ready, apprentice? Are you really that impatient?"

Kate shook her head. "It's just—"

"That you think you have learned enough for one day. You think that you know what is coming, or what is needed." Siobhan spread her hands. "Perhaps you are right. Perhaps you have mastered what I want you to learn."

Kate could hear the note of annoyance then. Siobhan didn't have the kind of patience as a teacher that Thomas had shown with her.

"I'm sorry," Kate said.

"It's too late for sorry," Siobhan said. "I want to see what you've learned." She clapped her hands. "A test. Come with me."

Kate wanted to argue, but she could see that there was no point to it. Instead, she followed Siobhan to a spot where the forest opened out into a roughly circular clearing bordered by hawthorns and brambles, wild roses and stinging nettles. In the middle of it, a sword sat, balanced across a tree stump.

No, not just a sword. Kate instantly recognized the blade that Thomas and Will had made for her.

"How…" she began.

Siobhan jerked her head toward it. "Your blade was unfinished, as you were. I have finished it, as I am trying to improve you."

The sword did look different now. It had a grip of swirling dark and light wood that Kate suspected would fit her hand perfectly. It had markings down the blade that were in no language she'd seen before, while now the blade shone with a wicked-looking edge.

"If you think you are ready," Siobhan said, "all you have to do is walk in there and take your weapon. But if you do, know this: the danger is real in there. It is no game."

If it had been another situation, Kate might have taken a step back. She might have told Siobhan that she wasn't interested, and waited a little longer. Two things stopped her from doing that. One was the insufferable smile that never seemed to leave Siobhan's face. It taunted Kate with the assurance that she wasn't good enough yet. That she would never be quite good enough to live up to the standards Siobhan set for her. It was an expression that reminded her too much of the contempt the masked nuns had shown her.

In the face of that smile, Kate could feel her anger rising. She wanted to wipe the smile from Siobhan's face. She wanted to show her that whatever magic the woman of the forest might possess, Kate was up to the tasks she set. She wanted some small measure of satisfaction for all the ghostly blades that had plunged into her.

The other reason was simpler: that sword was hers. It had been a gift from Will. Siobhan didn't get to dictate when Kate got to take it.

Kate took a run up and leapt to a branch, then jumped over the ring of thorns surrounding the clearing. If this was the best that Siobhan could manage, she would take her blade and scramble back out as easily as walking along a country road. She dropped into a crouch as she landed, looking across to the sword that waited for her.

There was a figure holding it now, though, and Kate found herself staring at it. At *herself*.

It was definitely her, down to the last detail. The same short red hair. The same wiry litheness. This version of her, however, wore different clothes, dressed in the greens and browns of the forest. Her eyes were different too, leaf green from edge to edge and anything but human. As Kate watched, the other version of her drew Will's blade, slicing it through the air as if testing it.

"You aren't me," Kate said.

"You aren't me," the other her said, with exactly the same inflection, exactly the same *voice*. "You're just a cheap copy, not half as good."

"Give me the sword," Kate demanded.

The other her shook her head. "I think I'll keep it. You don't deserve it. You're just scum from the orphanage. No wonder things didn't work out with Will."

Kate ran at her then, swinging her practice blade with all the strength and fury she could muster, as though she might break apart this thing with power of her attack. Instead, she found her practice blade met by the steel of the live one.

She thrust and she cut, feinted and beat, attacking with all the skills that she'd built up through Siobhan's brutal teaching. Kate pushed to the edges of the strength the fountain had granted her, using all the speed she possessed to try to break through her opponent's defenses.

The other version of her parried every attack perfectly, seeming to know every move as Kate made it. When she struck back, Kate barely deflected the strokes.

"You're not good enough," the other version of her said. "You'll never be good enough. You're weak."

The words rattled through Kate almost as much as the impact of the sword blows against her practice weapon. They hurt, and they hurt most because they were everything Kate suspected might be the truth. How many times had they said it in the House of the Unclaimed? Hadn't Will's friends shown her the truth of it in their practice circle?

Kate shouted her anger and attacked again.

"No control," the other her said as she deflected the blows. "No thought. Nothing but a little girl playing at being a warrior."

Kate's mirror image lashed out then, and Kate felt the pain of the sword cutting across her hip. For a moment, it felt no different from the ghostly blades that had stabbed her so many times, but this time the pain didn't fade. This time, there was blood.

"How does it feel, knowing you're going to die?" her opponent asked.

Terrifying. It felt terrifying, because the worst part of it was that Kate knew it was true. She couldn't hope to beat this opponent. She couldn't even hope to survive against her. She was going to die here, in this ring of thorns.

Kate ran for the edge of it then, casting aside her wooden blade as it slowed her down. She leapt for the edge of the circle, hearing her mirror image's laughter behind her as she threw herself at it. Kate covered her face with her hands, shutting her eyes against the thorns and hoping that it would be enough.

They tore at her as she plunged through them, tearing at her clothes and the skin beneath. Kate could feel the blood beading as the thorns ripped into her, but she forced herself through the tangle of them, only daring to open her eyes when she came out the other side.

She looked back, half convinced that her mirror image would be following, but when Kate looked, the other version of her was gone, leaving the sword sitting on its tree stump as if she had never been there.

She collapsed then, her heart hammering with the effort of all that she'd just done. She was bleeding from a dozen places now, both from thorn scratches and from the wound on her hip. She rolled to her back, staring up at the forest canopy, the pain coming in waves.

Siobhan stepped into her field of vision, looking down at her with a mixture of disappointment and pity. Kate didn't know which was worse.

"I told you that you weren't ready," she said. "Are you ready to listen now?"

CHAPTER FIVE

Lady Emmeline Constance Ysalt d'Angelica, the note read, *Marchioness of Sowerd and Lady of the Order of the Sash.* Angelica was less impressed by the use of her full name than by the source of the note: the Dowager had summoned her for a private audience.

Oh, she hadn't put it that way. There were phrases about being "delighted to request the pleasure of your company," and "hoping that it should prove convenient." Angelica knew as well as anyone that a request from the Dowager amounted to an order, even if the Assembly of Nobles made the laws.

She forced herself not to show the worry she felt as she approached the Dowager's chambers. She didn't check her appearance nervously or fidget unnecessarily. Angelica knew that she looked perfect, because she spent time in front of the mirror every morning with her servants, making sure that she did. She didn't fidget because she was in perfect control of herself. Besides, what did she have to worry about? She was going to meet one old woman, not walk into a shadow cat's den.

Angelica tried to remember that as she approached the doors to the old woman's chambers, a servant pushing them open and announcing her.

"Milady d'Angelica!"

She should have felt safe, but the truth was that this was the queen of the kingdom, and Sebastian's mother, and Angelica had done too much in her life to ever feel certain that she would avoid disapproval. Still, she walked forward, forcing herself to project a carefully crafted mask of confidence.

She had never had cause to be in the Dowager's private chambers before. To be honest, they were something of a disappointment, designed with a kind of plain grandeur that was at least twenty years out of date. There was too much dark wood paneling for Angelica's tastes, and while the gilt and silks of the rest of the palace were present in patches, it was still nowhere near the extravagance Angelica might have chosen.

"You were expecting something more elaborate, my dear?" the Dowager asked. She was seated by a window that looked out over the gardens, on a chair of dark wood and green leather. A marquetry table stood between her and another, only subtly less tall, seat. She was wearing a relatively simple day dress rather than full finery, and a circlet in place of a full crown, but there was still no doubt about the older woman's authority.

Angelica dropped into a curtsey. A proper court curtsey, not one of the simple things a servant might have bothered with. Even in something like this, the subtle gradations of status mattered. The seconds dragged out as Angelica waited for permission to rise.

"Please join me, Angelica," the Dowager said. "That is what you prefer to be called, isn't it?"

"Yes, your majesty." Angelica suspected that she knew very well what she ought to be called. She also noted that there was no corresponding suggestion of informality on the part of Sebastian's mother.

Still, she was pleasant enough, offering a raspberry tisane from a pot that had obviously been freshly brewed and serving Angelica a slice of fruited cake with her own delicately gloved hand.

"How is your father, Angelica?" she asked. "Lord Robert was always loyal to my husband when he lived. Is his breathing still poor?"

"It benefits from the country air, your majesty," Angelica said, thinking of the sprawling estates she was only too happy to stay away from. "Although he no longer rides to the hunt as much as he did."

"The young men ride in the vanguard of the hunt," the Dowager said, "while more sensible souls wait behind and take things at a pace to suit them. When I have attended hunts, it has been with a falcon, not a pack of charging hounds. They are less reckless, and they see more."

"A fine choice, your majesty," Angelica said.

"And your mother, does she continue to cultivate her flowers?" the Dowager asked, sipping her drink. "I have always envied her the star tulips she produces."

"I believe she is working on a new variety, your majesty."

"Splicing together lines, no doubt," the Dowager mused, setting her cup down.

Angelica found herself wondering at the point of all of this. She sincerely doubted that the kingdom's ruler had called her here just to discuss minor details of her family's life. If *she* ruled, Angelica certainly wouldn't care about something so pointless. Angelica barely paid attention when letters came from her parents' estates.

"Am I boring you, my dear?" the Dowager asked.

"No, of course not, your majesty," Angelica said hurriedly. Thanks to the civil wars, the days might have gone when the kingdom's royalty could simply imprison nobles without trial, but it still wasn't a good idea to risk insulting them.

"Because I was under the impression that you found my family fascinating," the Dowager continued. "My younger son in particular."

Angelica froze, unsure what to say next. She should have guessed that a mother would notice her interest in Sebastian. Was that what this was then? A polite suggestion that she should leave him alone?

"I'm not sure what you mean," Angelica replied, deciding that her best option was to play the part of the coy young noble girl. "Prince Sebastian is obviously very handsome, but—"

"But your attempt to sedate him and claim him for your own didn't go as planned?" the Dowager asked, and now there was steel in her voice. "Did you think I wouldn't hear about that little ploy?"

Now, Angelica could feel the fear inside her building. The Dowager might not simply be able to order her death, but that was what an assault like that on a royal person could mean, even with a trial of her noble peers. Maybe *especially* with them, since there would undoubtedly be those who wanted to set an example, or get her out of the way, or settle some score with her family.

"Your majesty—" Angelica began, but the Dowager cut her off with a single raised finger. Instead of speaking, though, she took her time draining her cup, then tossed it into the fireplace, the porcelain shattering with a crack that made Angelica think of breaking bones.

"An attack upon my son is treason," the Dowager said. "An attempt to manipulate me, and to steal my son into marriage, is treason. Traditionally, that is rewarded by the Mask of Lead."

Angelica's gut clenched at the thought of it. It was a horrific punishment from another time, and not one that she'd ever seen enacted. It was said that people killed themselves just at the thought of it.

"Are you familiar with it?" the Dowager asked. "The traitor is encased in a metal mask, and molten lead is poured inside. A terrible death, but sometimes terror is useful. And, of course, it allows for a cast of their face to be taken and displayed for all to see afterwards as a reminder."

She took something from beside her chair. It looked like just one of the many masks that were always around the court with the worship of the Masked Goddess. This one could have been the impression of a face though. A terrified, agonized face.

"Allan of Courcer decided to rise against the crown," the Dowager said. "We hanged most of his men cleanly, but with him, we made an example. I still remember the screams. It's funny how these things linger."

Angelica fell from her chair to her knees almost bonelessly, looking up at the other woman.

"Please, your majesty," she begged, because right then, begging seemed like her only option. "Please, I'll do anything."

"Anything?" the Dowager said. "Anything is a big word. What if I wanted you to hand over your family lands, or serve as a spy in the courts of this New Army that seems to be coming out of the continental wars? What if I decided that you should go and serve your penance in one of the Far Colonies?"

Angelica looked at that terrified death mask, and knew that there was only one answer.

"Anything, your majesty. Just please, not that."

She hated being like this. She was one of the foremost nobles in the land, yet here and now she felt as helpless as the lowest cottar.

"What about if I wanted you to marry my son?" the Dowager asked.

Angelica stared at her blankly, the words making no sense. If the other woman had said that she was giving her a chest of gold and sending her on her way it would have made more sense than this did.

"Your majesty?"

"Don't just kneel there opening and closing your mouth like a fish," the other woman said. "In fact, sit back down. At least *try* to look like the sort of refined young lady my son should be marrying."

Angelica forced herself back into her chair. Even so, she felt faint. "I'm not sure I understand."

The Dowager steepled her fingers. "There is little enough to understand. I am in need of someone suitable to marry my son. You are beautiful enough, from a family of sufficient standing, well connected at court, and it seems obvious enough from your little plot that you are interested in the role. It is an arrangement that seems highly beneficial to all concerned, wouldn't you agree?"

Angelica managed to collect herself a little. "Yes, your majesty. But—"

"It is certainly preferable to the alternatives," the Dowager said, her finger brushing the death mask. "In every sense."

Put like that, Angelica had no choice. "I would be happy to, your majesty."

"Your happiness is not my primary concern," the Dowager snapped back. "The well-being of my son and the safety of this realm are. You will not jeopardize either one, or there will be a reckoning."

Angelica didn't have to ask what kind of reckoning. Right then, she could feel the thread of terror running through her. She hated that. She hated this old hag who could make even something she wanted feel like a threat.

"What about Sebastian?" Angelica asked. "From what I saw at the ball, his interests are… elsewhere."

With the red-haired girl who claimed to be from Meinhalt, but who didn't behave like any noble Angelica had met.

"That will no longer be a problem," the Dowager said.

"Even so, if he's still hurt…"

The other woman fixed her with an even gaze. "Sebastian will do his duty, to both the realm and his family. He will marry who he is required to marry, and we will make it into a joyous occasion."

"Yes, your majesty," Angelica said, lowering her gaze demurely. Once she was married to Sebastian, perhaps she wouldn't have to bow and scrape like this. For now, though, she behaved as she had to. "I shall write to my father at once."

The Dowager waved that away. "I have already done so, and Robert has been delighted to accept. The arrangements for the wedding are already underway. I understand from the couriers that your mother fainted at the news, but then, she always was of a delicate disposition. I trust that it is not a trait you will pass to my grandchildren."

She made it sound like a disease to be expunged. Angelica found herself more annoyed by the way everything had just been put in place without her knowledge. Even so, she did her best to show the gratitude she knew was expected of her.

"Thank you, your majesty," she said. "I will strive to be the best daughter-in-law that you could hope for."

"Just remember that becoming my daughter buys you no special favor," the Dowager said. "You have been selected to perform a task, and you will do so to my satisfaction."

"I will strive to make Sebastian happy," Angelica said.

The Dowager stood. "See that you do. Make him so happy that he can think of nothing else. Make him happy enough to drive thoughts of… others from his mind. Make him happy, give him children, do all that the wife of a prince should do. If you do all that, your future will be a happy one as well."

Angelica's temper wouldn't allow her to let that go. "And if I do not?"

The Dowager looked at her as if she were nothing, rather than one of the greatest nobles in the land.

"You are trying to be strong in the hopes that I will respect you as some kind of equal," she said. "Perhaps you hope that I will see something of myself in you, Angelica. Perhaps I even do, but that is hardly a good thing. I want you to remember one thing from this moment on: I own you."

"No, you—"

The slap wasn't hard. It wouldn't leave a mark that would show. It barely even stung, except in terms of Angelica's pride. There, it burned.

"I own you as surely as if I had bought the indenture of some girl," the Dowager repeated. "If you fail me in any way, I will destroy you for what you tried to do to my son. The only reason you are here and not in a cell is because you are more useful to me like this."

"As a wife for your son," Angelica pointed out.

"As that, and as a distraction for him," the Dowager replied. "You did say you would do anything. Just let me know if you have changed your mind."

And then there would be the most horrific death Angelica could imagine.

"No, I thought not. You will be the perfect wife. You will be the perfect mother in time. You will tell me of any problems. You will obey my commands. If you fail in any of these things, the Mask of Lead will seem tame in comparison to what will happen to you."

CHAPTER SIX

They dragged Sophia outside, pulling at her even though she was walking under her own power. She was too numb to do anything else, too weak to even think about fighting. The nuns were delivering her on her new owner's orders. They might as well have wrapped her up like a new hat or a side of beef.

When Sophia saw the cart, then she tried to struggle, but it made no difference. It was a big, gaudy thing, painted like the wagon of some circus or troupe of players. The bars proclaimed it as what it was though: the holding wagon of a slaver.

The nuns dragged her to it and opened up the back, pulling back big bolts that couldn't be accessed from the inside.

"A sinful thing like you deserves to be in a place like this," one of the nuns said.

The other one laughed. "You think she's sinful now? Give her a year or two of being used by every man with the coin for her."

Sophia had a brief glimpse of cowering figures as the nuns threw the door open. Frightened eyes looked up at her, and she saw half a dozen other girls huddled on the hard wood. Then they shoved her inside, sending her tumbling among them with no room to gather herself.

The door slammed shut with a clang of metal on metal. The noise of the bolts was worse, proclaiming Sophia's helplessness in a scrape of rust and iron.

The other girls scrambled back from her while she tried to find a space there. Sophia's talent gave her their fear. They were worried that she would still be violent, the way the dark-eyed girl in the corner had been, or that she would scream until Meister Karg beat all of them, the way the girl with the bruises around her mouth had.

"I'm not going to hurt any of you," Sophia said. "I'm Sophia."

Things that might have been names were murmured back to her in the half light of the prison cart, too quiet for Sophia to catch most of them. Her power let her get the rest, but right then she was too wrapped up in her own misery to care much.

A day ago, things had been so different. She'd been happy. She'd been ensconced in the palace, preparing for her wedding, not locked in a cage. She'd been surrounded by servants and helpers, not frightened girls. She'd had fine dresses, not rags, and safety rather than the lingering pain of a beating.

She'd had the prospect of spending her life with Sebastian, not being used by a succession of men.

There was nothing she could do. Nothing but sit there, looking out of the gaps in the bars now, watching as Meister Karg walked out of the orphanage with a smug expression. He sauntered to the cart, then hauled himself up into the driving seat with a groan of effort. Sophia heard the crack of a whip, and she flinched instinctively after everything that had happened to her at the hands of Sister O'Venn, her body expecting pain even as the cart rumbled into life.

It crawled through Ashton's streets, the wooden wheels jolting as they found the holes between the cobbles there. Sophia saw the houses passing by at barely the pace of a walking man, the wagon in no hurry to get to its destination. That should have been a good thing, in a way, but it seemed then just like a way of drawing out her misery, taunting her and the others with their inability to escape the wagon.

Sophia saw people passing by, moving out of the way of the wagon only in the way that they moved aside for other large carts capable of crushing them. A few glanced at it, but they made no comment. They certainly made no move to stop it or to help the girls within. What did it say about a place like Ashton that this counted as normal?

A fat baker paused to watch them pass. A couple stepped back away from the tire ruts. Children were pulled close by their mothers, or ran up to stare inside on dares from their friends. Men looked in with considering expressions, as though wondering if they could afford any of the girls there. Sophia forced herself to glare back at them, daring them to meet her eyes.

She wished that Sebastian were there. No one else in this city would help her, but she knew that even after everything that had happened, Sebastian would throw the doors open and get her out. At least, she hoped he would. She'd seen the embarrassment on his face when he'd found out what Sophia was. Maybe he would look away too and pretend not to see her.

Sophia hoped not, because she could see some of what was waiting for her and the others, waiting in Meister Karg's mind like a toad for her. He planned to pick up more girls on his way to a waiting ship that would ferry them across the water to his home city, where there was a brothel that dealt in such "exotic" girls. He

32

always needed new ones, because the men there paid well for the chance to do what they wanted with the fresh arrivals.

Just thinking about it made Sophia feel nauseous, although maybe that had something to do with the constant rolling of the cart as well. Did the nuns know what they'd sold her into? She knew the answer to that: of course they did. They'd joked about it, and about the fact that she would never be free, because there would be no way for her to ever pay off the debt they'd imposed on her.

It meant a lifetime of slavery in everything but name, forced to do whatever her fat, perfumed owner wanted until she was no longer worth anything to him. He might let her go then, but only because it was easier to let her starve than to keep her. Sophia wanted to believe that she would kill herself before she let all of that happen to her, but the truth was that she would probably obey. Hadn't she obeyed for years while the nuns abused her?

The cart ground to a halt, but Sophia wasn't foolish enough to believe that they had reached any kind of final destination. Instead, they had stopped outside a hat maker's shop, and Meister Karg went inside without so much as a glance back at his charges.

Sophia rushed forward, trying to find a way to get to the bolts outside the bars. She reached through the gaps of the wagon's sides, but there was simply no way to reach the lock from where she was.

"You mustn't," the girl with the bruised mouth said. "He'll beat you for it if he catches you."

"He'll beat all of us," another said.

Sophia pulled back, but only because she could see that it wasn't going to do any good. There was no point in getting hurt when it wouldn't change anything. It was better to bide her time and...

And what? Sophia had seen what waited for them in Meister Karg's thoughts. She could probably have guessed it even without that there to make her stomach clench with the fear of it. The slaver's cart was not the worst thing that could happen to any of them, and Sophia needed to find a way out of it before it got worse.

What way, though? Sophia didn't have an answer to that.

There were other things she didn't have an answer to either. How had they found her in the city, when she'd managed to hide from hunters before? How had they known what to look for? The more Sophia thought about it, the more she was convinced that someone must have sent news of her departure to the hunters.

Someone had betrayed her, and that thought hurt worse than any of the beatings had.

Meister Karg came back, dragging a woman with him. This one was a few years older than Sophia, looking as though she had already been indentured for some time.

"Please," she begged as the slaver pulled her along. "You can't do this! Just another few months and I'd have paid off my indenture!"

"And until you pay it in full, your master can still sell it," Meister Karg said. Almost as an afterthought, he hit the woman. Nobody moved to stop him. People barely looked.

Or your master's wife can when she becomes jealous of you.

Sophia caught that clearly, understanding the horror of the situation in that moment through a combination of Karg's and the woman's thoughts. She was called Mellis, and had been doing well in the profession she'd been indentured to. Well enough that she'd been about to be free, except that the hat maker's wife had been sure her husband would leave her for the indentured woman as soon as she paid off her debt.

So she'd sold her on to a man who would ensure she was never seen again in Ashton.

It was a terrible fate, but it was also a reminder to Sophia that she wasn't the only one there with a harsh story. She'd been so focused on what had happened to her with Sebastian and the court, but the truth was that probably everyone had some sorrowful tale behind their presence in the cart. No one would be there by choice.

And now none of them would have a choice about anything they did in their lives.

"In," Meister Karg snapped, throwing the woman in with the rest of them. Sophia tried to press forward in the moments the door was open, but it slammed shut again in her face before she could get close to it. "We've a lot of ground to cover."

Sophia caught the flicker of a route in his thoughts. There would be more meandering through the city, picking up servants who were no longer wanted, apprentices who had managed to anger their masters. There would be a journey out of the city, into the outlying villages and as far north as the town of Hearth, where another orphanage waited. After that, there was a ship moored on the edge of the Firemarsh.

It was a route that would take at least a couple of days of travel, and Sophia had no doubt that the conditions for it would be awful. Already, the morning sun was turning the wagon into a space of heat, sweat, and desperation. By the time the sun reached its zenith, Sophia doubted she would even be able to think with it.

"Help!" Mellis called out to the people on the street. She was obviously braver than Sophia was. "Can't you see what's happening? You, Benna, you know me. Do something!"

The people there kept walking past, and Sophia could see how useless it was. Nobody cared, or if they did, nobody felt as though they could actually do anything. They weren't about to break the law for the sake of a few indentured girls who were no different from all the others who had been sold from the city over the years. Possibly, at least a few of those there had their own indentured servants or apprentices. Simply calling for help wouldn't work.

Sophia had an option that might, though.

"I know you don't want to interfere," she called out, "but if you take a message to Prince Sebastian and tell him that Sophia is here, I have no doubt that he'll reward you for—"

"Enough of that!" Meister Karg shouted, slamming the handle of his coachman's whip into the bars. Sophia knew what was waiting for her if she was silent, though, and she simply couldn't accept that. It occurred to her that the street people of the city might not be the right ones to ask for help.

"What about you?" Sophia called to him. "You could take me to Sebastian. You're just in this to make money, aren't you? Well, he could give you a profit on me easily, and you'd have the thanks of a prince of the realm. He wanted me for a fiancée two days ago. He'd pay for my freedom."

She could see Meister Karg's thoughts as he considered it. It meant that she shrank back the instant before the whip handle struck the bars again.

"More likely he'd take you and not pay a bent copper for you," the slaver said. "If he even wants you. No, I'll make my money off you the sure way. There's lots of men will want a turn on you, girl. Maybe I'll have a taste when we stop."

The worst part was that Sophia could see that he was serious. He was definitely thinking about it as the cart rumbled back into motion, heading into the outer spaces of the city. In the back of the cart, it was all Sophia could do to shut her mind to the prospect of it. She huddled down with the others, and she could feel their relief that it would be her and not them that the fat man chose tonight.

Kate, she begged for what seemed like the hundredth time. *Please, I need your help.*

As with all the other times, the sending went unanswered. It drifted off into the darkness of the world, and Sophia had no way of knowing if it even found its intended target. She was on her own, and that was terrifying, because alone, Sophia suspected that she couldn't do anything to stop all the things that were going to happen next.

CHAPTER SEVEN

Kate trained until she wasn't sure she could take any more deaths. She practiced with blades and sticks, fired bows, and threw daggers. She ran and she jumped, hid and killed from the shadows. All the time her mind was on the circle of trees and the sword that lay at their heart.

She could still feel the pain of her wounds. Siobhan had dressed the thorn scratches and the deeper puncture with herbs to aid healing, but they had done nothing to stop it hurting with every step.

"You need to learn to work through the pain," Siobhan said. "Let nothing distract you from your objectives."

"I know about pain," Kate said. The House of the Unclaimed had taught her that much, at least. There had been times when it had seemed like the only lesson the place had to offer."

"Then you need to learn to use it," Siobhan said. "You will never have the powers of my kind, but if you can touch a mind, you can distract it, you can calm it."

Siobhan summoned the ghostly forms of animals then: bears and spotted forest cats, wolves and hawks. They struck at Kate with inhuman speed, their claws as deadly as blades, their senses meaning that they could find her even when she hid. The only way to drive them off was to throw thoughts their way, the only way to hide from them, to soothe them into sleep.

Of course, Siobhan didn't teach her that with any patience, just had her killed again and again until Kate learned the skills that she needed.

She did learn though. Slowly, with the constant pain of failure, she learned the skills she needed the same way she'd learned to hide and fight. She learned to drive off the hawks with flickers of thought, and to still her thinking so thoroughly that it seemed to the wolves as though she was something inanimate. She even learned to soothe the bears, lulling them into sleep with the mental equivalent of a lullaby.

All through it, Siobhan watched her, sitting on nearby branches or following along while Kate ran. She never seemed to have Kate's speed, but she was always there when Kate was done, stepping from behind trees or within the shadowy recesses of bushes.

"Would you like to try the circle again?" Siobhan asked, as the sun rose higher in the sky.

Kate frowned at that. She wanted it, more than anything, but she could also feel the fear that came with it. Fear of what might happen. Fear of more pain.

"Do you think I'm ready?" Kate asked.

Siobhan spread her hands. "Who can tell?" she countered. "Do *you* think that you're ready? You find in the circle what you bring to it. Remember that when you're in there."

Somewhere in that, a decision had been made without Kate even realizing it. She was going to try the circle again, it seemed. Her still healing wounds hurt just at the thought of it. Still, she walked through the forest beside Siobhan, trying to focus.

"Every fear you have slows you down," Siobhan said. "You are on a path of violence, and to walk it, you must look neither left nor right. You must not hesitate, from fear, from pain, from weakness. There are those who will sit for years becoming one with the elements, or agonize over the perfect word with which to influence. On your path, you must *act*."

They reached the edge of the circle, and Kate considered it. It was empty save for the sword, but Kate knew how quickly that could change. She crept through the thorns, not disturbing the plants now as she slipped through them, moving silently into the circle. She slipped in with all the stealth she'd learned.

The other version of her was there waiting when she got through, the sword in her hand, her eyes fixed on Kate.

"Did you think that you could simply sneak in and take it?" the second self demanded. "Were you afraid to fight me again, little girl?"

Kate moved forward, her own weapon at the ready. She didn't say anything, because talking had done her no good last time. In any case, she wasn't good at talking. Sophia was better at that. Probably, if she'd been there, she would have already convinced the second version of herself to hand over the blade.

"Do you think that not talking does you any good?" her mirror image demanded. "Does it make you any less weak? Any less useless?"

Kate brought her weapon to bear, striking out high and low, keeping it moving.

"You've been training," her mirror image said as she parried. She struck back and Kate managed to deflect the blow. "It won't be enough."

She kept attacking and Kate gave ground. She had to, because the other version of her was exactly as fast, exactly as strong again.

"It doesn't matter how much you train, or how fast you get," her opponent said. "I will have all the same advantages and none of the weaknesses. I won't be a scared little girl, running from the pain."

She thrust at Kate, and Kate barely managed to dodge the worst of it, the blade cutting a line of fire along her ribs. Kate swayed back, cutting a wide slash with her practice sword in an attempt to keep the other version of herself at bay.

"Just a frightened, weak thing," her mirror self said. "How does it feel to know that you're going to die?"

Kate forced herself to smile. "You tell me."

She kept attacking, ignoring the fear, ignoring the voice that told her she wasn't enough.

"You're just trying to hide what you are," her other self said, although now there was a note that didn't sound as confident. Her parries weren't coming as fast either.

"You think I'm scared?" Kate asked. "You think I'm in pain? Let me show you what those *mean*."

She bundled it up then, all the pain that she'd felt in the House of the Unclaimed, all the fear that had come from being on the street alone. She took the hurt of not having her sister with her, and the loss of her parents, the fact that she'd had to leave Will. Kate took that pain and compressed it into a cannon ball of agony. She flung it at her mirror self.

The other her reeled back, clutching at her head. In that moment, Kate struck. Her practice blade was only wooden, so she didn't try to thrust it through the heart or open one of the big veins of the leg. Instead, she lunged with its tip for the throat, the wood slamming home and sending the mirror her sprawling.

"I am not weak," Kate said, striking again. "I have survived!"

The blade Will and Thomas had made tumbled from her opponent's hand. Kate snatched it up, testing the weight. The mirror self lay there, her hands scrabbling for the wooden sword, her eyes pleading for mercy.

Kate thrust the sword through her and she vanished.

For what seemed like forever, Kate stood there, breathing hard, her heart hammering in her chest. The blade in her hand had blood on it, and Kate wiped it clean with a handful of grass, trying to use the repetitive movement to calm herself. She could feel the grooves of the runes on the blade every time she passed over them, along with flickers of... something.

"You've done well," Siobhan said, walking through the thorns around the edge of the circle. They gave way for her like courtiers bowing out of the way of a queen. "You've pushed aside the things holding you back. The fear. The weakness. The mercy."

That last part scared Kate a little. She'd thrust her sword through the simulacrum without even hesitating. It hadn't been real, but even so, there had been blood on the sword. Kate might not have killed anything real there, but she had killed *something*. Guilt rose up in her with the inevitability of a rising tide.

"You say that as though it's a good thing," Kate said.

Siobhan put a hand on her shoulder. "You have sharpened yourself into the weapon you need to be."

"For what?" Kate asked. She should have guessed that there would be a reason why Siobhan would help her to become a better fighter. There had obviously been a reason why Siobhan had demanded a yet to be named favor as part of the price for her help.

Siobhan didn't answer. Instead, she tended to Kate's wounds, applying fresh herbs and cooling salve where they had opened.

"For what?" Kate repeated.

Siobhan stood, looking Kate in the eye. "There are things that are coming. Things that threaten those like me. You have seen an army coming, and you think that it is just a human kind of war. It is that, and many will die if you fail, but it is more, it is far more."

"How much more?" Kate asked.

"There are things in this world that destroy all they touch," Siobhan said. "This is not the time to talk about them."

That wasn't good enough for Kate. She wanted to reach out and grab the other woman. She wanted to demand real answers. She knew that she was being used; she just wanted to know in what way, and why. She wanted to have the kind of choice that had never been given to her back in the House of the Unclaimed. She would force an answer from the other woman if she had to. She would—

Kate! Help me!

The sound of Sophia's voice drifting into her mind stopped her like a hammer. On another occasion, she might have sent something back, or asked her to wait. Even now, a part of her wanted to stay and find out what was happening, but there was something about the feeling of her sister's sending that made her pause. She could feel Sophia's terror. She could hear the urgency in her words.

What is it? Kate sent back. *What's happening?*

There was no answer, just the original words, hanging there with all their terror.

"I... I need to go," Kate said. "Can I go? My sister is in danger. I know I'm supposed to stay here to be your apprentice, but—"

Siobhan raised a hand to cut her off. "I said that you were to be my apprentice, not that you needed to stay here, Kate."

"You're letting me leave?" That caught Kate more than a little by surprise.

That earned her the laugh of Siobhan's that said she was being foolish, or hadn't understood something, or was simply rushing into things again. Even in the short time she'd been the forest woman's apprentice, she had grown to hate that laugh.

"You were never a prisoner," Siobhan said. "You are free to make your own choices. Just know that they will have consequences, for all of us."

Still, Kate wasn't sure that she understood. "But if I'm your apprentice..."

"I am not your blacksmith," Siobhan said. "Do you think that I need you here to teach you? Wherever you are, you will still be my apprentice. Things will progress as they were always destined to progress."

Again, Kate had the sense of something larger going on in the background, but now there was no time to ask about it all, even if there was any chance that Siobhan might have told her.

"You will go out into the world," Siobhan said. "You will do what is necessary. You will learn, as you learned the first lesson: that you needed what I have to offer."

Kate swallowed at the thought of that, and the boy she'd killed. He'd deserved it, because he'd been trying to drag her back to the orphanage, but even so, Kate had been the one to end his life. Would all of Siobhan's so-called lessons come with that kind of a price?

"So I'm just going to learn from experience?" Kate asked.

"If I need to teach you more directly, that will be easy enough," Siobhan said. "I will summon you, and you will come. If I choose to, I might even come to you."

That caught Kate a little by surprise. She'd thought somehow that the other woman was limited to her woodland home. It meant something else as well: there would be no escape if she didn't keep her half of the deal that they'd made.

"Now," Siobhan said, "let's help you find your sister."

Kate hadn't thought about that part. Sophia would be back in the city somewhere, probably in or around the palace, but she had no way of knowing exactly where. The best she could do was call out to her with her powers and hope for a reply.

"You have a way?" Kate asked.

In response, Siobhan pulled out a needle like dagger, picking the pad of Kate's thumb and ignoring her wince of pain. She held Kate's thumb over a bowl until blood dripped into it, whispering words close enough that Kate couldn't catch them.

"Blood calls to blood," Siobhan said. "For a time, anyway. Move fast, and your blood will lead you to your sister. Move slowly, and you will be left searching for her."

"Then I'll have to move fast," Kate said.

She reached out, taking the bowl and cupping it like the precious thing it was. She kept it as level as she could, but even so, the drops of blood rolled to one side of the bowl. Kate barely had to look up to see that it was on the way back toward Ashton.

"We will see one another again, apprentice," Siobhan said. "For now, do what you are meant to do."

Kate didn't know how she felt about that. She didn't want to be bound by destiny any more than by the chains of another. For now, though, Siobhan had given her the means to find her sister, and Kate planned to make the most of it.

She ran, hoping all the while that she would be in time.

CHAPTER EIGHT

Sophia saw the moment when the city started to give way to the Ridings around it, in the thinning of houses and the changing pattern of bumps as the wheels hit more ruts. The forward progress made her fear build, because she knew all the things that were waiting for her when the cart stopped.

The old walls of the city had passed by a long time ago now, the continuing sprawl of houses meaning that there was no clean line stating where the city stopped. Briefly, Sophia found herself wondering what would happen if the wars over the water came to the kingdom. Would people find themselves trying to crowd behind the old walls, or just build barricades in the street? Would stone walls make a difference to cannon?

Then she realized that she didn't care. None of the people they passed tried to help her or the other girls. None of them looked at them with anything other than the contempt, useless pity, or dangerous interest that had been there since they'd started on this journey.

The cart was getting crowded now, because the slaver had made plenty of stops along the way. It seemed that there were a lot of people in Ashton who were prepared to sell servants or apprentices, foundlings or even daughters, not caring about what happened to them next. Perhaps they convinced themselves that the indenture was only temporary, and it didn't matter. Perhaps they didn't even consider it.

A pair of tough-looking guards joined them as they reached the edges of the city, riding on the outside of the wagon. Meister Karg might have felt safe enough driving around on his errands while there were houses, but now Sophia could pick up thoughts of forest cats and bandits, fathers having second thoughts about selling a daughter, or even rival slavers who might try to add to their stock without the work of trawling orphanages.

"Don't worry, my dears," Karg called down, in a cloying voice, as though he were talking to a clutch of beloved nieces rather than indentured slaves. "Hop and Burro here will see you safely to your destination."

Sophia doubted that the two men could deliver anyone unharmed. They were both broad and thuggish, with flat faces and pockmarked skin. They wore leather jerkins and dented breastplates, with poniards and basket-hilted swords at their belts. One even had a wicked-looking crossbow.

He winked at Sophia as she looked his way, his expression making it clear that she didn't want to look at his thoughts in that moment. She would probably never be able to scrub her mind clean again. The two rode at either side of the wagon, staring at the women within as often as at the road.

Sophia forced herself to ignore them, staring out at the road and the countryside beyond the city's sprawl instead. Maybe that was why she saw the figure running toward them first, and realized that it wasn't just some errand boy carrying a message from one of the farms beyond the outer rings of houses. This figure had a blade at its hip, and moved faster than Sophia would have thought.

More than that, it was familiar.

Sophia frowned, and for the first time since being thrown in the cart, she dared to feel some measure of hope.

"Kate?"

***

Kate sprinted forward, following the pull of the blood compass. When she saw the cart, the blood drop practically leapt from the bowl, falling to stain the dirt of the road a darker shade.

The cart looked like some kind of prison wagon. No, worse than that, a slaver. Anger burned in Kate then, and her hand tightened on the hilt of her sword, in spite of the guards clinging to either side of the wagon.

Sophia? she sent.

I'm here! Help!

That was all the confirmation Kate needed. She strode forward, and maybe she should have tried for subtlety, but right then she had no wish to even try to sneak or hide. Instead, she stood in the middle of the road, drawing her blade and waiting until the wagon drew to a halt in front of her.

"Out of the way, boy," the fat man driving it shouted down.

"I'm no boy," Kate shot back, "and you get one chance to live. Let everyone in that wagon go, and I won't kill you."

The two guards on the wagon stepped down. One pulled out a crossbow, leveling it at Kate.

"Little girls shouldn't make threats," he snapped. He glanced over to the fat man. "You want her for the wagon?"

The slaver shrugged. "Looks like too much trouble. Kill her."

The guard didn't hesitate. Kate saw the flicker of his thoughts as he made the decision to fire, and she'd spent enough time with Siobhan dodging spectral arrows to throw herself into motion, swaying aside as the bolt buzzed past. It thudded into the dirt of the road, burying itself almost to its fletching.

"Thank you," Kate said, turning back to them, "for making this easy."

They ran at her then, and Kate stepped between their rush, dodging the slash of a broadsword and the thrust of a long knife. She brought her own blade up, parrying another thrust, swaying aside from a wide sweep and kicking one of the thugs' feet from under him.

"You're not very good at this, are you?" she asked.

One of the men roared and ran at her, trying to overwhelm her through sheer strength. Kate stood there, her feet rooted to the ground, feeling the strength of the forest flooding through her as she parried every stroke. The man pressed closer and she kicked him in the knee, then ducked a blow aimed by the second thug.

Kate flicked her wrist and her sword danced out to cut his throat. She'd thought it would be harder to do, but the blood pulsing beneath his skin seemed to want to jump clear. She was just clearing the way for it.

While he fell, the first thug attacked her with all the fury of a man who didn't have anything else. Kate gave ground, stepping aside from his attacks neatly, then lunged. The sharp tip of her saber slid through the gap between his plate armor and the leather behind it, finding the flesh beneath. Kate heard his gasp as she pulled it clear.

She advanced on the slaver, and he scrambled from his seat, pulling out a whip and a knife. Kate stared at the whip with anger. She'd felt enough beatings in her life already.

"I gave you a chance," she said. Her anger had turned into something so hot it looked cold now, the way metal could go from red hot to white. She floated on it as she advanced. "You could have lived."

"I'll break you," he promised. "Do you think I haven't broken wild little things before?"

"I'm sure you have," Kate said. "Why don't you try?"

He swung the whip, and Kate didn't even bother to step inside the arc of it. Instead, she lifted an arm, ignoring the pain as it struck, letting it wrap around her forearm. She jerked, pulling the slaver forward in spite of his bulk. With him moving, all it took from her was to hold out the sword she held. She barely even felt the impact as it slid into his heart.

It was only in the aftermath of it that Kate started to feel again. She watched him fall, and the adrenaline of the fight started to rush out of her. She forced herself to move slowly, cleaning her sword and sheathing it. The sense of horror she'd had when she'd killed the boy from the orphanage was there, but it was less this time. These men had deserved it.

The main thing she felt was exhilaration, at her strength, at her speed. She was everything she could have hoped for. Siobhan's tests should have shown her that, but this, *this* was the real proof of it.

She moved to the doors of the slave wagon, throwing them open and letting sunlight rush in. Sophia was the first to come out, wrapping her arms around Kate and looking at her in astonishment. Kate clung onto her.

"Thank you," Sophia said. "I thought…"

"It doesn't matter," Kate said. "You're safe now."

It felt good to have her sister there. It felt *right*. Kate wished they could stay there like that forever.

"Thanks to you," Sophia said. "They were going to sell me."

"What happened?" Kate asked. "Did your prince do this?"

If he had, Kate would kill him. No one would do this to her sister and get away with it. No one who could do this should be allowed to go around with the chance to do it again.

"No!" Sophia said, and Kate could feel the shock there. "Sebastian would never do something like this. No, this was the House of the Unclaimed. They found me; I don't know how, but they did. They whipped me in the courtyard and they sold me off to the highest bidder."

Kate felt her anger flaring again. She looked at Sophia's dress now, seeing the blood that stained it. The House of the Unclaimed had fallen from her attention in the time she'd been Thomas's apprentice, and then Siobhan's. Now, it filled her thoughts.

She watched while girls and women spilled from the slaver's cart. They came out blinking in the sunlight, looking scared and happy in equal measure. Kate could tell that they weren't certain what to make of the things that were happening to them. Most of them had resigned themselves to their fates, and now their entire futures had changed.

Kate went to the slaver and his thugs, pulling the weapons from their belts and pressing them into the hands of the women there.

"You're free," she said. "I'm not going to tell you what to do now, but I do know that eventually, someone will come looking. If you stay here, they'll sell you again at best, hang you at worst. You can go and hide in the city, or go find families if you have them. You can take to the roads or build lives."

It was a hard message, but someone had to tell them. She felt Sophia's hand on her shoulder.

"My sister is right," she said. "You're free now, and I don't know what that means next, but it means *something*. It means that you have a chance of something better." She turned to Kate. "I'll find a way to explain it to them, and then... what do we do after that?"

"We'll think of something," Kate said. "Can you stay here with them for a while?"

"Why?" Sophia asked, and Kate caught the note of suspicion there.

Kate looked back toward the city. "There's something I need to do before we leave."

***

Kate ran into the city, sprinting through the outskirts and along the narrow streets, hopping across the rooftops where it was quicker, and staying out of sight of the crowds below. She used the skills of stealth and agility now as a way to keep from having to answer questions or make up lies.

She had no time to be slowed by those around her. She was an arrow now, flung at her target by an invisible hand. An arrow that would bring vengeance, but also one that would free those who lay within her target.

It lay ahead. Kate would have recognized the House of the Unclaimed even if she'd left it a thousand years to come back, and now it stood out against the rest of the city in its squat ugliness. It looked like the prison it was in all but name. She thought about those within. The thought of the children trapped there made her burn with the need to free them. The thought of the nuns who had hurt her and Sophia...

...that just made her burn with anger.

Kate hopped down to street level, walking to the front gates that sat open to taunt those within with a freedom they could never truly have. Inside, there were candles waiting for the evening, the sconces filled by some child's unwilling hands. Kate took one, ignoring the looks of the masked nun by the gate as she lit it.

She walked through the orphanage, and something about the purpose with which Kate did it kept people there back from her. Very deliberately, she walked to the chapel, where the symbols of the Masked Goddess were set out, the nuns murmuring in fervent prayers before cloths set with her symbols, drapes of the finest silk hanging around the walls.

"What are you doing here?" one of the nuns asked, rising. In spite of her veil, Kate recognized Sister O'Venn. After a moment, it seemed that the masked nun recognized her too. "You!"

"Yes," Kate said. "Me."

There were a thousand clever things she could have said. A thousand comments listing all the harm the nuns had done. A thousand wrongs to right. She could have demanded answers for what they'd done to Sophia. She could have told them that she was some kind of divine retribution, come to settle with them for what she'd done. She could even have asked them if they were proud of her, because weren't the orphans there *supposed* to go on to apprenticeships and indentures?

In the end, none of it seemed adequate, so Kate set her candle to the drapes and stepped back as they caught, the sheets of silk turning into sheets of fire.

"What have you done?" Sister O'Venn demanded. "You evil girl, I'll make you beg to be sold before I'm done with you!"

Kate cocked her head to one side, waiting. The nun was bigger than her, but it didn't make any difference once Kate drew her sword.

"What are you going to do with that?" the masked nun demanded. "Evil child! You'll hang for this, or worse!"

"You've already done worse," Kate said, "to me and plenty of others."

She swung her sword, taking a slice from the nun's arm while stepping aside from the nun's attempt to grab her. She didn't cut deep, not yet. Sister O'Venn, of all of them, didn't deserve the mercy of a quick death. Kate sliced at her leg, then whirled away, ripping away the mask with a cut of the saber that revealed a blunt face beneath.

Kate kept cutting, slicing the nun apart a piece at a time, one cut for every wrong, every stroke of the whip, every declaration that she and the others were evil, worthless things. When the sister collapsed to one knee, Kate didn't stop, because her rage wouldn't let her. Sister O'Venn deserved this, and a thousand times worse than this. Around the room, the flaming drapes continued to burn, the fires rising higher.

"You should beg *me*," Kate said. "Beg for a quick death. Beg!"

"Please…" Sister O'Venn managed.

Kate kicked her back. "No."

The other nuns were screaming by then, in a way they hadn't when Kate had started the fire. They ran for the door, and Kate cut at them almost at random as they passed. She didn't have enough time to pick through them for the ones who had hurt her, and in any case, just by what they'd done there, they'd hurt *someone*.

She stalked from the chapel, slamming the door behind her. It was the easiest thing in the world to slip a bolt into place, ignoring the screams from within. They deserved this, as surely as one breath followed another. Kate wished she had time for individual revenge against each of them. She had children to free, though. She made her way out into the orphanage while the smoke poured from the room behind her.

"Run!" she yelled to the children there. "This is your chance! Go!"

Some of them ran. More of them didn't. Many of them cowered back from Kate as though worried she might kill them, when she would never do anything to hurt them.

"Run!" she bellowed, glowering at them. If she couldn't get them to safety through kindness, maybe she could do it through fear. More ran now, running away from the sight of her stalking through the compound there.

Kate made her way through the House of the Unclaimed's rooms, opening them one by one to release those within. Most of them looked at her in confusion as Kate pulled them away from the cranks or the grinding wheels and pushed them toward the door. Occasionally, there were nuns there, driving their charges on with canes or straps. Kate shoved them out of her way, and now only the ones who tried to attack her died. That first rush had done a lot to sate her need for violence.

When Kate saw that some of the boys who liked to beat the others were there, though, her hatred surged back into life. One of them ran at her, and Kate hit him with the hilt of her blade, the metal coming away bloody.

"What's wrong?" Kate demanded. "Isn't it as easy when people aren't helpless?"

She hit him again, sending him sprawling, then kicked the legs of another from under him. The boys turned and ran. Kate let them go, because she had more important things to do. Freeing the others was what mattered now.

At least, it was until she shoved open another door and found a masked nun beating one of the girls there. Her back was already bloody with it, but still she kept going.

"Evil thing! How dare you question the will of the Goddess? The one who ran deserved her punishment, and you will share it until you repent!"

Instantly, Kate found herself thinking of her sister. One look at the nun's thoughts and Kate had no doubt that this girl was suffering because she'd dared to question Sophia's punishment. She also had no doubt that she was no better than Sister O'Venn, enjoying the pain just as much.

Kate smashed into her from behind, knocking her face first into the wall. Kate grabbed the lash as it fell from the nun's hand, striking out with it and catching her across the face. Kate hit her again, ignoring her screams. If she'd had enough time, she would have beaten the woman until there was nothing left of her. Instead, her sword lashed out, and she fell headless.

"Hold on," Kate said, working to untie the girl. "I'll cut you free."

She was a little taller than Kate, thickly built and plain, with sandy blonde hair and dark eyes. Kate thought that she vaguely remembered her from lessons. They hadn't been friends, or enemies, or anything really. They hadn't even known one another. Why would this girl stand up for Sophia?

"What's your name?" Kate asked.

"Rosalind," the girl managed. "And you're Kate, aren't you?"

Kate nodded. "Hold on, I'm going to get you out of here."

"And go where?" Rosalind asked.

Kate hadn't worked that part out yet, but it didn't matter. She cut the girl down and helped her to stand. "We'll find somewhere. Come on."

She could have kept going in the House of the Unclaimed. She could have happily stalked it, killing every one of those who had tormented her. Instead, she propped up Rosalind, making for the door to the orphanage, leaving the House of the Unclaimed burning behind her.

CHAPTER NINE

Sophia waited for Kate even when the other girls left, melting off into the fields in ones and twos, heading off to whatever lives they might be able to find for themselves. She pushed down her worry about what might happen if anyone came looking for the slave wagon. If anyone came, she could hide, but she wasn't going to leave the one spot where she might find Kate again.

Sophia worried as she waited. She worried about the possibility of travelers or watchmen walking by and seeing the wagon. She worried about the smell coming from the corpses of Meister Karg and his thugs, dragged to the side of the road where Sophia and the others had managed to pull them out of sight, looting them for the coin that they had stowed, ready to pay for more girls.

Above all, she worried about Kate.

Would she be safe on this errand of hers? More than that, what was she doing? Sophia had seen the look in her sister's eye when she'd left, and it had done nothing to reassure her. There was a hardness to Kate that Sophia guessed had always been there, but now it seemed to have been strengthened, turned into something more dangerous.

Even so, Sophia waited. She wouldn't abandon her sister.

As she waited, she searched the wagon. There was a chest there, and Sophia broke it open, hoping to find gold that she and Kate could use. Instead, she found provisions, documents, even gaudy-looking clothes that she guessed were there in case the slaver wanted to show his charges off in something more than ragged shifts. Sophia went through them until she found a plain shirt, a dark skirt, and a jacket that was sewn with glass beads that might pass for jewels in poor light. It was an improvement on what the House of the Unclaimed had forced her into, at least.

When Kate appeared, she did so running down the road with a speed that was almost shocking. Sophia could see the blood on her, and she had to steel herself to reach out and grab for her sister. Had to remind herself that Kate would never hurt her.

"Kate, what happened?" Sophia demanded. "Are you hurt?"

When Kate shook her head, Sophia could feel the satisfaction there.

"Not me," she said. "The people who tried to stop me. And there was a girl, Rosalind. She was hurt. I had to get her to safety."

"What happened, Kate?" Sophia asked. She thought about the bodies of the slaver and his men, how easily Kate had killed them all. "What did you do?"

"What I had to. I've stopped the House of the Unclaimed from hurting more people."

Sophia's response to that wasn't what she might have thought it would be. She was happy that the place was gone, if it really was, and there was a sense of relief that the horrors of the place were over. At the same time, she couldn't help worrying about the blood that flecked her sister's tunic, and the ease with which she'd killed people in front of her.

"What did you do there?" Sophia repeated.

"I burned part of it," Kate said, with more than a hint of satisfaction, "I set the children free. I killed Sister O'Venn, and some of the others."

Again, Sophia could feel conflicting emotions rising up though her. She could share Kate's satisfaction at the news that the masked nun who had tormented her was dead. She wasn't going to whip any more indentured girls until they couldn't stand. She wasn't going to sell anyone else off, as cruel as the slavers she supported. At the same time, Sophia was worried that Kate had been the one to do it, chasing vengeance ahead of anything else.

"Where did the others go?" Kate asked.

Sophia shook her head. "I don't know. I don't think they wanted to risk staying here. What happened with the girls from the orphanage?"

"They scattered into the city," Kate said.

Sophia could hear the disappointment there. She could understand it too. A part of her had hoped that the other women from the slaver's cart would stay near her, because they were safer together than apart. Sophia didn't want to guess what might happen to them. She hoped that they would be all right, but given the way Ashton was, there were no guarantees.

"We have each other, though," Sophia suggested. It was more of a hope than a reality. She hugged her sister to her, and they moved away from the road, where there was no chance of being seen. Now, Sophia wasn't so much worried about the chance of people catching them as about the violence that Kate would bring to bear if they did.

"So," Kate asked when they were clear of the road, "are you ready to tell me how you ended up in a slaver's cart? You were at the palace."

Sophia swallowed at the thought of it all. So much had happened in such a short space of time that it was hard to fit it into her head.

"I was going to marry Sebastian," she said. "But... he found out who I was. He said that his family would never allow the marriage."

"He sounds like a fool," Kate said. "I should find him for you, and—"

"No," Sophia said hurriedly. "Don't even think it. Don't talk about him like that." She was surprised to feel the anger there behind the words. "I knew what the dangers were when I started pretending."

"He could have accepted you anyway," Kate said. "But he didn't."

He hadn't, and then the House of the Unclaimed had taken her off the streets. Sophia wasn't sure which part of that hurt more.

"What about you?" she asked. "Where... how did you learn to fight like that?"

"I found someone in the forest," Kate said. "She knows things that... she knows about people like us. She agreed to teach me."

"To be a warrior," Sophia said. It wasn't that she disapproved of the decision, because she knew that Kate had always been fascinated by that side of life, but even so, there were so many other things she could have done. "I thought you were going to be a blacksmith."

"Things went wrong," Kate said. "Will, the blacksmith's son... he joined one of the free companies, and when I went to see them, they beat me senseless. The House of the Unclaimed came close to grabbing me too. I couldn't stay. Siobhan was the only one who could help me."

"Maybe she could help me," Sophia joked. "Turn me into a great warrior too."

She expected a laugh from her sister at the sheer absurdity of it all. Instead, Kate's expression turned serious, and Sophia could feel an edge of hardness under the surface of her thoughts.

"You wouldn't like her training methods," Kate said. "And it's not just fighting. She gives people what they want."

Kate managed to make that sound more like a curse than a benefit.

"What is it you want?" Sophia asked her. "What are you planning to do now? What are you going to do with all this strength you have?"

She half hoped that her sister would be ready to walk away with her, finding somewhere safe away from Ashton.

"Will's company humiliated me," Kate said without hesitation. "I'm going to go back and teach them better."

Sophia probably should have guessed that was the kind of thing her sister would want to do. Even so, she couldn't help a note of disappointment.

"Revenge?" Sophia asked.

"Yes," Kate admitted. "I'm going to make them pay."

Sophia shook her head, reaching out to put a hand on her sister's shoulder.

"You don't have to," she pointed out. "You could just walk away. You know that you're stronger than them. You could go and do some good with the strength that you have. You could be happy."

"I'll be happy when I see them sprawled in the dust after they've tried to fight me again," Kate shot back.

"Why?" Sophia asked. "What's so great about revenge? Did it feel so good when you were burning an orphanage? When you were killing people?"

"Yes," Kate said, and there was a hardness to her now that frightened Sophia a little. "Yes, it did."

How was it that they could be sisters and still be so different? It made no sense to Sophia, this chasing after vengeance, no matter what it cost. Her first instinct on hearing that the ones who had hurt her were dead was satisfaction, but she'd also been worried for her sister. She still was.

"Vengeance isn't everything," Sophia said. "You can't build a life on it. You have to have more."

"What matters more?" Kate countered. "If I can't have revenge, what else can I have?"

There was love, and happiness. There was the prospect of a safe life, where she didn't have to fight every moment just to survive. Sophia wanted to offer it all to her sister, but she knew Kate too well for that. Kate was set on her course, and there would be no deflecting her from it.

"What about you?" Kate asked. "What do you want?"

"I want..." Sophia had been going to say something about a home or a life, but the truth was that there was only one thing she truly wanted. "I want to go to Sebastian. I want him to know that I

54

wasn't just tricking him so that I could marry a prince. I want him to know that I really loved him."

"And then he takes you back?" Kate asked. "Just like that?"

Sophia shook her head. Kate was missing the point there. Maybe it was one that she couldn't understand, as focused as she was on her revenge.

"It's not about persuading him to take me back," Sophia said. "I just want him to know the truth. I want him to understand that it wasn't a lie when I told him I loved him. Once he knows that, it doesn't matter about being a part of the court anymore. I've seen what that means. I can just leave and start a new life. *We* could."

"It sounds as though you're as caught up with love as I am with revenge," Kate said.

Sophia smiled at that. "Is it such a bad thing to be caught up with?"

It was better than revenge, wasn't it?

"What's the point of telling him that you love him?" Kate demanded. "What does it *do*?"

"Maybe nothing," Sophia admitted, "but I have to try."

"It's bad enough when it puts you in other people's hands," Kate said. "You give all you are to someone, and then when it goes wrong, you're left vulnerable. At least with my way, there's no one left to hurt us afterward."

Sophia hated hearing her sister talk like that. She pulled her closer.

"We could just leave," she said. "All the others from the wagon have gone off to find new lives. Why couldn't we? We could go past the Ridings, through the Shires, maybe go as far as one of the smaller towns. We could do it together."

"It sounds like a lovely idea," Kate said. "And we'll do it when this is done."

"But?" Sophia prompted.

She heard her sister sigh.

"But we both have things that we want to do first," Kate said. "That we *need* to do. We can do them, and then meet up."

"Once you've had your revenge," Sophia said.

She watched as Kate shrugged.

"Not just that. I have to finish my training. I have to repay the blacksmith who took me in. And his son…"

"What about his son?" Sophia asked. Kate's blush gave her the answer. Kate *never* blushed.

Her sister plowed on at a speed that said it was meant to be a distraction. "After that… maybe I'm strong enough that I don't

55

need to go and hide in the woods anymore. Maybe I can actually build a life."

Sophia could understand that now. She didn't feel the same need that she'd had to make it into the castle, regardless of what happened to her. She'd thought that a place at court was the best way to survive, but now she could see that it had as many dangers as anywhere else. She just wanted to be loved, and to be safe. Those weren't things that were too much to ask.

Were they?

"It feels as though we did this once before," Sophia said. "It didn't work out so well then."

"We want different things now," Kate pointed out. "And things have changed, for both of us."

"I'll still be there for you if you need me," Sophia said.

"And I'll be there for you," Kate replied. "I was today, wasn't I?"

Sophia nodded. Kate had been there for her, although it had taken a night of screaming for help to bring her. And when she'd come, the death that had followed in her wake had left Sophia feeling guilty for being the one to ask for her help. It was one reason they couldn't walk the same path now, any more than they could before.

"Just promise me that you'll be safe," Sophia said as she stepped back from Kate.

Kate drew her sword, slicing it through the air with the speed of a striking snake.

"I'll be safe," she said. "No one can hurt me now."

Sophia hoped that was true. She knew there were far more ways to hurt someone than simply beating them in battle. She hoped that Kate didn't end up learning that the hard way, because she'd felt that pain.

It was one reason she had to go her own way now. She had to find Sebastian. She had to undo some of the damage that had come from her unmasking. She had to at least let him know how much she loved him, even though she knew it could never lead to anything. She couldn't do all that while following Kate along on her mission for vengeance.

In truth, she didn't want to watch that side of her sister either.

"So, this is it?" Sophia said, stepping back from Kate.

"Not forever," Kate replied. "Not even for long. I'll do this, you'll talk to your prince, and we'll meet up. It will be a day at most."

Sophia nodded. Not forever, just for now. They would find one another again. They were connected in a way that meant that they would never truly be alone. Even so, as Sophia set off back in the direction of the city, it hurt to leave her sister behind.

Love was worth it, though, if anything was.

CHAPTER TEN

It was a long walk for Sophia back to the palace, not least because she spent most of it looking around, trying to make sure there was no one following her. With every step now, she expected someone to make a grab for her. After all, it had happened before.

It meant that, by the time she reached the palace, her nerves felt as tightly strung as a harp, leaving her glancing around at every noise as she made her way up to the gates. She tried not to think about the way she looked. The clothes she'd taken from the cart were better than the shift from the orphanage, but she doubted she looked much like the noble she'd been pretending to be anymore.

It didn't help that her back was still in agony, and the long walk from the outskirts of the city hadn't improved things. She wasn't sure what it would look like if she collapsed on the steps of the palace, but Sophia doubted that it would be good. She wasn't sure, given how dirty and worn she must look then, that anyone would even let her in.

Her heart fell at that thought, and at the sight of the guards at the gates, but it rose again quickly enough. She recognized one of the guards there as the one who had been sent by Sebastian to follow her into the city when she'd gone to meet her sister.

"Hello," she said. "I'm surprised to see you on the gate."

"We go where we're sent, my lady," the guard said. Sophia could pick out the surprise in his thoughts at the way she looked, but he wasn't thinking about her as some kind of intruder. News of what had happened hadn't gotten around the palace yet.

Prince Sebastian will want us to treat her with courtesy, Sophia heard, picking the thoughts out with her talent. She dared to relax, just a little. Perhaps this could work.

"I'm here to see Sebastian," she said.

"Yes, my lady," the guard said. "May I ask what this is about? You were not expected."

How could Sophia answer that? If she told the man that she was there to declare her love for the prince, then he would probably laugh at her, or assume that she was just one more in a parade of young women petitioning the royal family for attention. She knew it happened often enough with Rupert. Probably the guards were used to turning girls away by now once *he* was done with them, even if Sebastian wasn't anything like the same.

"I just need to see him," Sophia said, trying to make it sound as though she had the confidence of nobility, and didn't need guards telling her where she could go.

Perhaps it even worked, because the guard stepped back to let her inside without asking more questions.

He turned as she moved to go in. "I should say, my lady, that Prince Sebastian isn't here. He left the palace this morning and hasn't come back yet. If you wish to wait for him, though, I am sure no one will mind."

Sophia was sure that there were plenty of people who would mind, but she went to do it anyway. Disappointment rose in her that Sebastian wasn't there, because she wanted to talk to him now, here, before she lost the courage to do it.

She could wait, though. She *would* wait. She would go to Sebastian's rooms and be there when he got back. Even if he asked her to leave again, at least that way she would have a chance to tell him just how much she loved him.

Sophia set off through the palace, and was a little surprised by how easily she found her way through it now. She'd gotten used to it in the time she'd spent with Sebastian. She'd learned to fit in there, even if really, she'd never felt as though she belonged. If some of the servants she passed looked at Sophia with surprise, she didn't mind. The important thing was that she was going to see Sebastian again.

There were other people Sophia was less eager to speak with.

Milady d'Angelica was standing outside Sebastian's rooms, with the look of someone trying to appear to be merely passing, but who had been standing there for some time. She was resplendent in a cream and gold dress that had been cut to flatter her, in stark contrast to Sophia's simple clothing. Sophia tried to pull back into an alcove, but she didn't move fast enough to avoid Angelica's gaze.

"What are you doing here?" Angelica demanded, making no attempt to disguise her dislike. "Especially looking as though you've stolen your clothes from a brothel."

Sophia forced herself to remain civil at least. The way to deal with the likes of Angelica was not to rise to their provocation.

"I'm here to see Sebastian," she said, as calmly as she could.

Angelica sniffed. "And *what* would you have to say to my fiancé?"

That last word seemed to fall onto Sophia like a stone.

"Your… no, I don't believe it," Sophia said. "You're lying."

"Believe what you like," Angelica said. "But the marriage is being arranged as we speak. That's the way things are done among *civilized* people."

Sophia wanted to say that it was a lie again, but she'd met the Dowager, and the circle in which she moved. She knew how things were done amongst the kingdom's noble families, and beyond. She'd made a point of learning so that she could play the part of the displaced noble, on the run from the wars across the water.

"Sebastian wouldn't agree," she tried.

"To a marriage to someone so suitable?" Angelica countered. "You know how Sebastian feels about doing his duty. And I promise you, this is one duty he will enjoy doing."

The worst part was that Sophia could see it. Sebastian had put her aside because of his duty, hadn't he? Didn't it make sense that he would do this if his duty demanded it too? And Angelica was right about the rest too. She was suitable. She was nobly born, intelligent, beautiful, and elegant. The part where she was also cruel and calculating didn't come into it. It possibly even counted in her favor, in Ashton.

"The truth hurts, doesn't it?" Angelica said.

It hurt more than Sophia could have imagined. Worse than the pain in her back. Worse than any of the losses that she'd suffered, because it felt as though it closed off a door in a way that it couldn't be opened again. Sophia fought against the tears that threatened to spring into her eyes, but she didn't know how long she would be able to keep them at bay.

"To think I thought you were a threat," Angelica said. "Look at you. Just a weak, broken thing in a dress that doesn't even fit her."

"I'll—" Sophia began, but the truth was she didn't know what she would do. If she'd been Kate, probably she would have hit Angelica then. If she'd been the noble she'd been pretending to be, she would have brought the weight of her connections and her position to bear. As it was, she could only stand there.

"What will you do, Sophia of Meinhalt? If that's even your name." Angelica smiled over at her. "Why don't you go? Run along." Her expression turned ugly. "*Run,* or I'll have you dragged from here and thrown into the gutter, where you belong."

Sophia ran, and not just because Angelica told her to. She ran because she couldn't face the situation in front of her. Because the thought of Angelica with Sebastian was just too terrible to face. She ran because she really *didn't* belong there, and she'd been stupid to believe that she ever could.

She ran blindly, partly because the tears made it hard to look where she was going, and partly because Sophia didn't have anywhere to go right then. She ran deeper into the castle, not caring that she didn't know where she was running to.

"Lady Sophia?" a woman's voice called, and the familiarity of the voice stopped Sophia. She looked around and found herself staring at Laurette van Klet, the artist whose painting had ruined the façade she'd worked so hard to produce. She stood there, dressed in an artist's smock, paint flecking her hands as though Sophia had caught her in the middle of painting a new work.

Sophia stood staring at her, torn between the urge to run again and the desire to step forward and slap her for doing so much to help ruin Sophia's life. Everything had been perfect until Laurette had spotted the mark of Sophia's indenture.

"Are you all right?" Laurette asked.

How could Sophia answer that? She couldn't, and she turned to go again, because there was nothing for her here.

"Wait," Laurette called. "Please don't go."

Sophia stopped. "Why?" she asked. She thought for a moment. "What are you even doing here? I thought Sebastian sent you away."

"He did," she said. "But I didn't get far. I wanted to speak to you."

"If it's about what you painted, it's too late to change it," Sophia snapped.

She saw the artist frown. Sophia was too upset to begin to sort through the woman's thoughts, but the confusion seemed genuine.

"Why would I change it?" she asked. "I paint what's there."

Sebastian had said much the same thing. That it was the artist's gift, and her curse. It had been the reason he'd sent her away to paint in the high hills of the northern mountains.

"If it's not that, then what?" Sophia demanded.

"I saw something," Laurette said. "And I thought you should see it too. I'm sorry, you're upset. People tell me that I should notice these things more."

She passed Sophia a handkerchief that had probably been a very fine thing before paint had gotten onto it. Even so, it was a moment of kindness, and those had been few and far between in the last day or two.

"Will you come with me?" Laurette asked. "I have something to show you."

Sophia went with her, following along into rooms that Sophia recognized. They'd held paintings when she and Sebastian had gone there. Now, they just held a forest of bare easels, waiting in expectation to be filled.

"Most of my things are still packed away," Laurette said. "Tell me, do you think Sebastian will want me to paint for his new wedding too? I know he sent me away, but I think he was just angry at what was happening."

"I... don't know," Sophia said, managing to keep a grip on her temper only because it was obvious that the artist's mind didn't work in quite the way other people's did. "You said that you had something to show me."

"Yes, yes, of course," Laurette replied, going over to a bag that was more like a sack with handles, filled with art supplies and old canvases. She started to sort through them, picking out one wrapped in paper against the possibility of it being damaged in transit. She took it out and started to unwrap it, setting it on one of the easels.

"What am I looking at?" Sophia asked.

"I stopped at the Marquis of Bruthel's estate last night," Laurette said. "And of course he wanted to show me his paintings. And... well, look."

The painting she placed on the easel showed a man and a woman in early middle age, wearing what looked like expensive but slightly out of date clothes. Sophia recognized their features instantly, because she saw those faces in her dreams every time she went to sleep. The shock of that was enough to keep her staring.

"Those are my parents," Sophia said, unable to keep the excitement out of her voice.

"You're sure?" Laurette asked. "I wanted you to see the painting because I saw the resemblance, but also because... they didn't want me to see this. They said they shouldn't show me, but I told him I wanted to study the brush strokes, and I told him I'd restore a spot where it has faded."

Sophia frowned at that. "Who said it?"

"The Marquis," Laurette said. "He said he shouldn't even have the painting, but it was too good to destroy. A Hollarde, he said. The former royal painter, before the civil wars."

The wars again. They seemed to have shaped every aspect of the kingdom as it stood now, turning it into something that was neither one thing nor another, caught between different sides in a constant dance that seemed to hurt everyone else.

"Do you know who they are?" Sophia asked, looking at the painting for any clues. The man looked strong but kind. The woman was beautiful and poised, with the same features Sophia saw whenever she looked into a mirror. She needed to know. She could tell Kate. Sophia was sure her sister would want to know even more than she did. After all, she'd carried the locket with her mother's picture around for years.

Laurette nodded and turned the picture over, reading from a label. "Lord Alfred Danse and his wife, Christina, at their estate in Monthys, on the occasion of his lordship's fortieth birthday."

It looked more like a formal occasion than a celebration to Sophia, but that part barely mattered then. All that mattered was finding out the truth.

"Monthys?" she asked.

"It's in the north," Laurette said. "In the foothills of the mountain lands. I went close to there once, to paint watermills."

"You're sure?" Sophia said. "I suppose I could check in the library."

"No," Laurette said, and Sophia caught the sense of panic behind it. "No, you mustn't."

It's too dangerous. Doesn't she know?

"Know what?" Sophia asked, and only then realized what she was doing. "You're acting as if it's dangerous, Laurette."

"It is," she said. "Lord Alfred and Lady Christina were important people, and... I don't know if they're alive now, but the Marquis was afraid even to mention them. They were so close to the throne, and now... now it's as though they were never alive at all."

"Close to the throne?" Sophia said.

Laurette shook her head, but her thoughts gave it away.

Their children might have inherited if not for the wars, if not...

Shock hit Sophia with that thought. If her parents had royal blood, then *she* had royal blood, and so did Kate. The idea of it seemed preposterous, the world seeming to spin under her.

"Are you all right?" Laurette asked.

"I'm just... I'm trying to make some kind of sense of this," Sophia said.

It *didn't* make sense. She was just a girl from an orphanage, playing at being a noblewoman. The idea that she might really be everything she claimed was ludicrous. How could that have happened? How could she have ended up in the House of the Unclaimed?

The answer to that came to her in memories of flames and the need to run.

Sophia knew what she had to do then. She had to go north. She had to find Monthys, and learn the truth of all this. It struck her as the kind of thing Kate would have jumped at, and maybe she still would, but Sophia knew she was the one who had to do it. Kate would have loved this. She would have seen the thought of a trek across half the country as an adventure. Sophia was the one who had to make the journey, though, and she would do the best she could.

"What will you do now?" Laurette asked.

"I… I guess I'll try to find out the truth," Sophia said.

"Just be careful," the artist replied. "You know, the Dowager wants me to paint for the new wedding, regardless of how Sebastian feels. I think that will feel strange. Have you met Milady d'Angelica?"

"Yes," Sophia said tightly. "I've met her."

"I don't think she'll be as good a sitter as you," Laurette said. "Good luck, and… I'm sorry that I caused so much trouble for you."

Sophia shook her head. "That wasn't you," she said. "It was my stupidity."

Now, though, maybe she had a chance to make up for it. Maybe she could find a way to make this right. Maybe she could find out the truth.

She set off through the palace, determined to get going and find a way north. She made her way through the corridors of the palace, and it was only when a hand closed over her shoulder that Sophia realized she hadn't been as careful as she should have been.

"And just where," Prince Rupert asked, "do you think you're going?"

CHAPTER ELEVEN

Sebastian thought he knew all about Ashton, but it wasn't until he toured it trying to find Sophia that he got a true sense of how large it was. He found himself stalking down every alley on horseback, hunting through every square for some sign of her.

Where would she go after what had happened? After all he'd done to hurt her?

Sebastian's feelings felt like some tangled sailor's knot, and it was that knot that kept him walking the city, stopping at every flash of red hair or glimpse of a face that seemed faintly similar.

It was only when he started to hear the rumors about the House of the Unclaimed that Sebastian started to get a sick feeling in his stomach. The orphanage had been burned, everyone within slaughtered. Packs of children were on the streets, running and stealing. If Sebastian hadn't known about Sophia's past, he wouldn't have connected her to it. Now…

What had he done, turning her away like that? He'd done what duty demanded, what his family would have demanded, had they known. There was no way he could have been with Sophia without the risk of bringing the whole monarchy crashing down. The Assembly of Nobles would never have stood for a marriage between him and one of the indentured.

Right then, none of that mattered. Sebastian wanted to at least see Sophia again, even if he didn't know what he wanted to do when he did. He still had the ring he'd given her, and that she'd let fall to the carpet when she'd left. He knew he couldn't offer her that in marriage, but he still had it tucked away in the pocket of his tunic, against the moment when he might meet her again.

He hurried down toward the House of the Unclaimed, hoping that he was right, and that he would have the chance to see Sophia once more before his regiment demanded his presence for the wars that seemed to be growing ever closer. Sebastian had heard about the New Army sweeping through the continent, brushing aside Disestablishers and Free State men alike, absorbing mercenary companies and local forces even as it destroyed them. Sebastian felt a spark of fear at having to go to fight that, but it was nothing compared to the worry he felt for Sophia right then.

That worry only grew as he saw the area around the House of the Unclaimed. This was where Sophia had been brought up? These streets full of filth and violence had been the ones she had known as a child? It was bad enough that anyone had to live in such poverty, let alone that Sophia should.

"Please don't let her have been in there," Sebastian said when he finally saw the state of the orphanage. His horse whickered in response. The thought that Sophia might have been inside the place felt as though it was about to tear a hole in him. He wouldn't be able to forgive himself if she was gone.

Even from the outside, he could see how much of it had been damaged by the fire, and there were watchmen milling around the entrance, obviously trying to make sense of it as they pulled bodies from the building. Some brought buckets, dousing the last embers of the fire, while others stood and asked questions of anyone who strayed close to them.

"What happened here?" Sebastian asked, riding up to one of the men and dismounting.

The watchman turned with the expression of someone who had been asked that question too many times already today.

"Why don't you run along before I... wait, you're Prince Sebastian."

The change in the man's demeanor would have been comical in its suddenness if it hadn't been in such a terrible situation. As it was, Sebastian didn't care about anything except whether Sophia was all right.

"What happened here?" Sebastian repeated, putting whatever authority he could muster into it. In truth, his brother Rupert was better at that kind of thing, but then, Rupert enjoyed the power that came with being royalty.

"Nothing to worry about, your highness," the man said.

Sebastian shook his head. "I'll be the judge of that. Or do you want me to tell my mother that I couldn't find out what she wanted to know?"

It was a lie, but probably a useful one, given his mother's reputation for wanting to know all the workings of the city. Sebastian saw the man swallow.

"The Dowager wants to know?" he said. "Oh, goddess... sorry, your highness. I just meant that this is a terrible business. We're still getting the details from the survivors. It seems that an escaped girl was recaptured last night and punished for it."

"Punished?" Sebastian said. He knew they had to be talking about Sophia. If they'd hurt her... no, they *had* hurt her, and the anger of that flamed through him, barely under control. If he hadn't been standing in front of the ruins of the orphanage, he might have stormed in there himself.

"She was whipped and her debt was sold on," the man said as if it were nothing, "but then the girl's sister came and... well, that's the part that doesn't make much sense."

"Tell me," Sebastian said, forcing himself just to listen, not to react to what he knew was news of the woman he loved being tortured and sold into slavery. It was harder than he could have believed. He could feel himself physically shaking with the effort.

"Well, they say that the girl's sister walked in, set light to the orphanage, and single-handedly killed half the nuns and priests there. It just doesn't sound likely. The nuns are used to subduing unruly children."

"With whips, apparently," Sebastian said, unable to keep the sharpness out of his voice. Was he the only one there who saw something wrong with that? Who saw the cruelty in whipping young people whose only crime was to have no home? Looking at the bodies being dragged from the orphanage, he saw that all of them were adults. Again, he could feel conflict rising, because on the one hand there was the horror that came from seeing this kind of cold-blooded carnage. On the other, if these people had played any kind of role in harming Sophia, Sebastian would have gladly killed them himself.

"What about..." He wanted to say Sophia, but stopped himself. "What about the girl they recaptured? Is there any sign of her?"

"No, your highness," the watchman said, in a careful tone of voice probably reserved for explaining things to his betters. "This wasn't that girl. This was her sister. They call her Kate."

Sebastian took it slowly. "And I'm assuming that she acted as she did because she couldn't find her sister. So what happened to the first girl? If I wanted to find her, where would I do it?"

"Probably halfway to one of Karg's brothels by now," another man said.

Sebastian whirled, his fist closing ready to throw a punch. Only the kind of control that came from long years around his brother stopped him. "What did you just say?"

"I was just asking the nuns," the second watchman explained. "That was who bought the sister's debt, a slaver named Karg." The watchman spat, seemed to realize who he was talking to, and paused. "I figured that the girl who did this might go after him, but they'll be on the high road out of the city by now and—"

Sebastian was already remounting his horse and had it in motion before the other men were finished staring at him in surprise. They didn't matter. Only Sophia mattered.

He thundered toward the high road, hoping that he wouldn't be too late, steering his horse around the carts and the wagons there, heading out of the city in a blur of passing buildings and shouted insults as he rode too fast. He rode out into the scattered outskirts of Ashton, where there was more room to give his horse its head.

Even so, Sebastian held back. There was only so far he could go. His regiment would be waiting for him, and if he didn't arrive by the time it was ready to embark, he would be deserting it. For someone who wasn't a prince, that would mean the noose, but even for him it would mean disgrace.

Next to finding Sophia, did disgrace really matter?

So he kept riding. He rode until he saw the cart, abandoned by the side of the road. He rode around until he found the bodies, and Sebastian could guess what had happened. Sophia was gone, escaped with the help of her sister. Joy and disappointment hit him at the same time. Joy, because it meant Sophia was free. Disappointment because there was no chance of him finding her now.

He didn't spare the slaver a thought. If anyone had deserved death, it was this man. He traded in cruelty. What did it say that his mother's kingdom allowed it at all?

He felt... empty as he rode back in the direction of the city. Deadened by the loss. He didn't push his horse now, because he'd already done that too much today. Instead, he let it walk at its own pace, while he tried to sort out some of what he felt. Sebastian suspected would take more than one journey to do, because there were simply too many emotions to deal with. He'd lost Sophia again, and now she could be anywhere.

Sebastian turned off the main road, taking one of the smaller paths that would lead to the training grounds. His regiment would be waiting, and he had no more time.

He almost didn't see the girl walking along the road until it was too late. If it hadn't been for her flame red hair, Sebastian might not have noticed her at all. That caught his attention, though, because it was the same shade as Sophia's, and there was something about her features that was almost the same, even if this girl was shorter, and dressed more like a boy.

When she saw Sebastian, she stepped back from the road and all but disappeared in the nearest bushes. If Sebastian hadn't seen her there on the road, he wouldn't have believed that there was anyone there at all.

"Hello?" he called, drawing his horse to a halt. "Is someone there? You don't need to be afraid. I'm not going to hurt you."

The girl stepped out. There was a sword in her hand that looked wickedly sharp, leveled at Sebastian's heart.

"No," she said. "You aren't."

"Are you Kate?" Sebastian asked. The guess felt so natural, so obvious, that he couldn't help but make it. She looked so similar to Sophia that it seemed impossible that she could be anyone else.

"Yes," the girl answered. "And you're Sebastian, the scum who cast out my sister for the masked nuns to take."

Shock hit him at being spoken to like that. More importantly, how had she guessed that? Maybe she'd seen his face on a portrait somewhere.

"It wasn't like that," Sebastian said.

"No?" Kate didn't look convinced. "You told Sophia that she wasn't good enough for you, and the next thing any of us know, she's being snatched by the House of the Unclaimed. Are you telling me I *shouldn't* cut your heart out?"

She took a step forward with a determination that suggested she meant it. Again, Sebastian was more than a little surprised at being spoken to like that. Normally, people were polite to him, even obsequious.

"It feels as though someone already did," Sebastian replied. As if they'd taken it out and stamped on it, leaving nothing but pain behind. "Is Sophia safe, at least? I swear I had nothing to do with her being taken."

Kate looked at him for several seconds. "No, you didn't, did you? Except for the part where you threw her out. I should still kill you for *that*."

Sebastian wondered if she could actually do it. He was a long way from helpless, even if he didn't take the kind of joy in battle that Rupert and some of the other nobles did.

"Draw your sword if you want to try," Kate said.

Sebastian shook his head. "I saw what you did at the House of the Unclaimed. I saw what you did to the slaver's men."

He heard Kate snort. "Those weren't men, and at the orphanage... they deserved it."

"For what they did to Sophia? They did," Sebastian said. He could agree with that much, at least.

"For what they did to all of us," Kate said, her tone still combative. "Does this mean that you're not planning to drag me off to justice, *your highness*?"

She somehow managed to turn even that into an insult.

"Look," Sebastian said. "I know that you hate me for what happened with your sister, but I was just trying to do my duty. I loved her. I *love* her. Can you... can you tell her that, if you see her?"

"Maybe," Kate said with a shrug. "You *could* go and tell her yourself."

She sheathed her sword. It seemed that she wasn't going to kill him today. Sebastian didn't know whether to feel relieved or robbed.

Sebastian shook his head. "There's no more time. I have to get to my regiment."

On impulse, he took the ring from his pocket. He tossed it to Kate, and she snatched it out of the air with the speed of a striking snake.

"What's this?" she asked.

"It was her engagement ring," Sebastian said. "I want her to have it. I want her to know that I love her even if... even if who I am makes it impossible to be with her. She can keep it, or sell it if she needs the money, or... just make sure that she gets it?"

To his surprise, Kate nodded without arguing. She took a chain from around her neck, on which a locket sat, adding the ring to it.

"When I see her, I'll give it to her," she said.

"Thank you," Sebastian replied.

"I'm not doing it for you," Kate said. "I'd gut you if I weren't certain that it would break her heart. And I could, whatever you think."

Perhaps she could. Given what was coming, maybe that was a talent Sebastian should have been trying to make use of.

"Have you considered joining one of the regiments?" he asked. "I know they don't usually let in women, but mine will, if I—"

"Do you think I have any interest in taking orders from you?" Kate asked.

Sebastian guessed that she wouldn't. She wasn't the same as her sister, no matter how much the two of them looked the same.

"You could be an asset in the war, Kate," he said.

He saw her shrug.

"Maybe," she said. "But right now, there's only one regiment I'm interested in."

CHAPTER TWELVE

Kate was thankful she wasn't going in the same direction as Sebastian. She could see that he loved Sophia, but that still didn't make things around him any simpler. If she'd had to follow him all the way to the training grounds, it would have been difficult, deciding what to do next.

As it was, Sebastian soon turned off the path, heading for whatever royal regiment he was serving with. The truly rich didn't serve with the free companies. They served with the historic regiments, or they owned their own companies. It made things simpler in a lot of ways. Kate doubted that Sophia would be happy if Sebastian got caught up in her revenge.

"An interesting young man."

Kate jumped at the sound of Siobhan's voice, then stepped back in shock as the woman of the forest stepped out from behind a tree by the road.

"How did you do that?" Kate asked.

Siobhan smiled in response. "Maybe I didn't. Maybe this is all an illusion. Or maybe I can reach out to touch any forest. Maybe there are ways to walk, if you know them."

"Are there?" Kate said. The idea of paths that could go anywhere was an impressive one.

"That is not the path you chose," Siobhan reminded her. "You chose to become a thing of violence. I was just wondering how that felt. How did it feel when you killed the ones who had tormented you?"

Kate wasn't sure how to answer that. It had felt good at the time. It had felt like exactly the thing she needed to do, and she still felt good about the children she'd freed from the place's cruelty. Even so, there was something frightening about the speed with which she'd killed so many people.

"Are you having second thoughts?" Siobhan asked.

"Would it make any difference if I were?" Kate countered. "I drank from the fountain. I owe you a favor. Is that what this is? Are you here to ask for it?"

She saw the other woman shake her head.

"Not yet," Siobhan said. "I'm merely checking on you, my apprentice. Ensuring that you're happy with the choice you made. Checking that you want the destiny it leads to. If you aren't... well, perhaps we could find another path for you. I've told you some of the other things you could learn."

She had, and some of them were impressive. More than impressive, they seemed like the stuff of dreams. It was just that they weren't *her* dreams. She couldn't imagine herself as the kind of witch Siobhan was, even if they'd been the same kind of thing to start with. No, the training Siobhan had given her felt like the right thing, even if the path it led on was a bloody one.

Maybe especially then.

"This could be your last chance," Siobhan said.

"This is the thing I want to do," Kate replied.

Siobhan smiled at that. "Then go do it. Become all you must be."

She stepped back behind her tree, and when Kate followed to look for her, she was gone, as surely as if she'd never been there.

At least talking to Siobhan had clarified things. She wanted this. She wanted revenge on the company that had humiliated her. She couldn't let this lie.

Kate set off again, walking onto the training ground.

There were plenty of men there, training with blades and bows, working with the bulky iron of cannon and beating dents out of armor. Men sat and diced or drank, but it seemed to Kate that there were fewer of them than there had been the last time she'd been there. There was a sharper edge to things now. They were getting ready for war.

Kate could feel the eyes on her as she walked through it all. She wondered how many of those there recognized her. Probably most of them, because the pain of her humiliation certainly burned through her with every glance. Kate could feel the expectation in their thoughts, waiting for more entertainment from the girl who wanted to be one of them.

She would entertain them, all right.

Kate made her way to the training ring where they'd had a boy beat her senseless before, and she could hear the sound of clashing blades there. That was good. She wanted someone to fight.

When she got there, though, what she saw made emotion bubble up in her.

Will stood in the center of the ring, a blunted practice steel in his hand. Two others faced off against him, moving around him like sharks waiting to strike. Every time he turned to one of them, the other jumped forward to strike, battering Will about the legs and ribs.

If this had been a friendly bout, any one of those blows would have stopped it and forced them to reset. Even training with Siobhan, there had been a break every time an insubstantial weapon had plunged through her. It had been designed to be a lesson, even if it was a cruel one.

This was just a punishment.

Kate had no doubt that it was for bringing her there, because she couldn't imagine Will breaking some other aspect of the discipline there. The blows that rained onto his body, overseen by the same soldier who'd put her in the ring with the bigger boy, were just a way of inflicting pain.

Kate couldn't allow it.

She charged forward, stepping in behind one of the two there and tripping him so that he fell face down in the dirt. She snatched his blade away and threw it at the second with stunning accuracy, catching him on the temple so that he stumbled and fell.

She reached out for Will, and he took her hand, standing.

"Kate?" he said. He sounded both happy to see her and worried. Worried that this would make things worse, for both of them. "What are you doing here? It isn't safe."

"I don't care about safe," Kate said. "I *do* care about you."

She drew her wooden blade for the moment, but that wasn't kindness, just the desire to hurt them with the same tool that they'd used to hurt her.

The veteran who had arranged her beating the last time she'd been there stepped forward. Around them, men started to gather, obviously sensing the chance for some more entertainment at Kate's expense.

"Didn't you learn your lesson the last time?" the veteran asked.

"Oh, I've learned plenty of lessons," Kate said. She pushed Will gently back out of the way. "Why don't you come and find out?"

He laughed at that. So did most of the men there. They were obviously expecting another beating, another easy victory.

The veteran pointed to two men. "I don't have time for this. Johan, Gerald, teach this girl a lesson. If she wants to be a camp follower, maybe we'll make her into one. Beat her senseless and then you'll get the first go with her."

Two men moved forward, reaching for Kate, not even bothering with blades. She stepped back away from the first, swinging her wooden blade at his head. He moved to make a parry, and Kate dropped the practice sword low, striking his knee in a crack of wood.

She spun, ducking on instinct as the second swept a punch at her head. Kate rolled as the first man limped toward her, then came up and jabbed the tip of her practice blade into his belly, driving the air out of him in a whoosh. She brought her knee up sharply as he doubled over, snapping his head back as she knocked him into unconsciousness.

The other man ran at her, trying to close the distance and grab, but Kate wheeled away, then leapt, jumping over his head as he lumbered toward her. She struck down in midair, feeling the crunch of wood against bone as she struck the base of his skull. He tumbled into the dirt as easily as the first man.

"As I said," Kate said, rising up from the crouch in which she landed, "I've learned since last time."

"Tricks and nonsense," the training master snapped back. "They mean nothing when there's blood at stake."

He stepped forward, drawing a broad-bladed sword with a basket hilt. It looked like a cleaver compared to the elegance of Kate's own weapon.

"You've come here twice now," he said. "I'll not have you doing it a third time. I'll see you dead." He pointed past her. "You and the idiot who brought you here."

Kate drew her real blade then. No one threatened Will while she was around. If this man wanted blood, she would give him blood.

"Let me show you how much I've learned," she said.

The soldier was fast, and he was skillful. He lunged in with an attack, then shifted lines, dipping his point under Kate's sword as easily as if his weapon had been some light fencing blade. Kate had already picked the move from his mind, though, and her sword moved down to meet the attack.

She gave ground, circling her opponent.

He cut again, trying another feint. Kate slipped back from this one, the point of her weapon cutting across his forearm in a line of crimson.

"We can stop if you want," Kate said. "Isn't that what noblemen do? They fight to first blood because they don't want to die."

She was goading him, and he took the bait.

"One wound doesn't make a fight," the soldier said. "And I'm no noble. I'll gut you, wench. I'll watch you die slow."

He tried to make good on his threat, battering at Kate's defenses, trying to break through using sheer force. It might even have worked if Kate had tried to block the blows, because her weapon wasn't solid enough to withstand that kind of assault. She kept moving instead, dodging back from the strokes, slipping inside the line of them, all the while watching her opponent's thoughts for the next trace of violence, the next trick he'd try.

She cut his tunic open next, scoring another line of blood across his chest, then managed to cut into his cheek as she disengaged from his attempt to bind her blade. Kate dodged a charge, kicking the soldier into the dirt, then cut across his thigh almost as an afterthought as he stood.

It seemed that he'd had enough then, because he turned to the other men there. "Don't just stand there! Get her!"

Men ran forward, and now Kate found herself at the heart of a storm of flashing blades and clubbing fists. It was far harder to simply avoid the flow of the attack now, and Kate found herself having to parry and jump, lean and keep moving in order to stay ahead of it. The training Siobhan had put her through helped, and Kate found herself responding faster than she ever could have before it.

She didn't hold back. These men were trying to kill her, and she saw no reason not to return the favor. She took pain and flung it into the thoughts of the nearest men, then thrust through one of their chests. She parried the swing of a rapier and her saber cut back across a throat. Around Kate, the world narrowed into a thing of movement and violence, every instant bringing a fresh threat that needed to be dealt with, the sweep of a blade or the thrust of a dirk at her ribs.

Kate fought with her sword and with her body, striking out with kicks as she spun, cutting at unprotected flesh. She deflected a sword cut and sliced into an arm, then kicked behind her to connect with a man whose thoughts of sneaking up she caught. She pushed aside a man who ran in to grab at her, then leapt clear, seeking out the training master she'd been dueling with.

He saw her and looked around as if considering running. Instead, Kate felt him ball up his fury, building it into something that came out as a roar as he charged at her. He cut and struck, forcing Kate to give ground with every attack. There was no cleverness to this, no strategy, just violence.

Kate let him come, then left the tiniest of openings. Her opponent lunged at her then, aiming for her heart, but Kate was already moving. She swayed aside, feeling the blade slice across her shirt without ever touching the flesh beneath.

Her saber found its mark though. It sliced into her assailant's neck, cutting through as he stared at her in surprise. He stumbled past her a step or two, sheer momentum carrying him past Kate, as if he didn't understand what had just happened to him. The sheer sharpness of Kate's saber might have had something to do with that. It had felt like almost nothing as it struck, and now Kate stood there, watching him fall.

The other soldiers stared at their officer as he died, then at her. They backed away in obvious confusion, and Kate could feel their fear of her. She had to admit then that she probably looked fearsome, with the blood of her opponents on her, and no wounds marring her in return.

After a lifetime of being beaten and pushed down, it felt good to be the one people were scared of for once, rather than someone they chose as a victim. She felt strong. She felt dangerous.

Not dangerous enough to deal with what happened next, though.

Men came up from all sides, some armed with crossbows, some pikes. There were even a few blunderbusses, their trumpet mouths unwavering as they targeted Kate. This was more than she'd faced in any of her training with Siobhan, and more than anyone could hope to dodge. Presumably, Siobhan's answer to this would be not to be here.

Kate didn't have that option. She stood there, waiting for them to fire; waiting to die. She let her sword clatter from her hands, because there was nothing that she could do with a sword to counter the storm of projectiles that would follow.

Men came forward, and even though Kate wasn't moving now, she could feel their fear. They had shackles in their hands, and part of her wanted to fight, wanted to knock them down for trying to contain her. She forced herself to stay still while they fastened the shackles to her wrists, dragging her away from the scene of the carnage while Will watched, held in place by another of the men there.

"Lord Cranston says we can't execute anyone without his orders," one of the soldiers said. "But once he gets here, girl… you'll hang for this."

CHAPTER THIRTEEN

Sophia stopped as Rupert's hand rested on her shoulder, the strength of his grip enough to keep her pinned in place regardless of anything she might want. The sight of the prince should have probably made her think of fairytales, because he was golden-haired and handsome enough for any of them. Instead, it just made her afraid.

"Lady Sophia," he said in a courtly tone, moving to stand before her. "I'm so glad that I caught you before you left us."

Caught was the word, and Sophia could see from his thoughts that he'd meant it quite literally. He saw her the same way that he might see a doe running before his hounds: as something to be run down for the sport of it.

"Your highness," she said, forcing a smile and remembering to adopt the accent she'd used as Sophia of Meinhalt. "It is good to see you again. You look very dashing today."

"And you are a vision of loveliness," he said, looking her up and down in a way that made Sophia squirm in discomfort. "I was sorry to hear that things had not gone well between you and my brother."

He wasn't sorry at all; Sophia could see that he was all but reveling in it, enjoying both Sebastian's failure to marry her and her sudden availability. Especially that.

"You're very kind, your highness," Sophia said.

Rupert laughed at that. "Oh, I'm anything but kind, but I find that isn't what people want. Is it, Sophia?"

He used her name as familiarly as if he'd known her for years.

"I like kind people," Sophia said. "The world is too full of cruelty."

"The world is what it the Masked Goddess made it," Rupert said. "A place of the hunter and the prey, of blood, strength, and steel. There is an excitement in that, don't you find?"

He didn't know that Sophia's story was false. From what he knew, she was fleeing a war, and yet he still talked about it as though it was an adventure. It was either thoughtless or deliberate cruelty. Sophia suspected that it was the latter.

"I've had more than enough of that kind of excitement, your highness," she said.

Rupert blinked. "It's a rare woman who disagrees with me," he said. "Still, maybe we can discuss it more, over wine."

"I'm sure that would be wonderful," Sophia said. She would make any promise she had to, if it let her get out of there. "Perhaps this evening?"

"Now, I thought," Rupert said, his hand fastening onto Sophia's wrist. He was still smiling, but there was no warmth in it. "Unless you have something better to do?"

His thoughts said that he was enjoying her discomfort, and Sophia guessed that he would take any refusal as an insult. At a point when she wasn't even meant to be there, Sophia knew that she couldn't afford the kind of scene that might follow if they argued.

"One drink," she said, hoping that by the end of it, she would have found a way to extract herself from Rupert's grip. She could see that it wasn't drinking that was on his mind. The things that were made her want to recoil, but she could see that Rupert was waiting for that. He wanted to chase her.

Help, she sent, hoping that Kate would hear. Hoping that she would come, even as Sophia wished that she had an option that didn't involve calling for her sister every time there was trouble.

"Come," Rupert said, and from the outside it must have looked as though he'd merely taken her arm to escort her. They passed by a servant, and Rupert snapped his fingers. "Have wine brought to my rooms. The Westmarches Gold, I think."

"Yes, your highness," the servant said, and even though she looked at Sophia with sympathy, she made no move to interfere.

"I've changed my mind," Sophia said, hoping that the servant would get the message that she didn't want any of this. "I'm sorry, but I have a prior engagement, and I can't stay for wine."

"Nonsense," Prince Rupert said, and now his grip tightened on Sophia's arm enough to hurt. He turned to the servant. "Run and fetch the wine."

The servant hurried off, and Rupert kept his painfully tight grip on Sophia's arm.

"Please, your highness," she begged. "You're hurting me."

"Yes," he replied. "I am. Disobedience must be punished, or how will obedience be learned? This kingdom understood that once, before the civil wars. A ruler could give commands and expect them to be obeyed. You *will* obey me, won't you, Sophia?"

Sophia swallowed. "What would you have me do, your highness?"

Prince Rupert stared at her, and his grip tightened again. "Oh, all kinds of things. For now, though, I would like to hear the words. Say them."

Sophia wondered that he would do this to someone he thought was a noblewoman. Yet, to Rupert, she was just a refugee with no family, completely at his mercy. The worst part was that she *was* at his mercy, and the House of the Unclaimed had taught her that there was only one thing to do in that situation.

"Yes, your highness, I will obey you."

Rupert seemed pleased by that. "I look forward to learning if that is true."

Please, Sophia sent again, *help me.*

There was no sign that Kate had heard, and Sophia doubted that she would be able to get there in time even if she did. In the orphanage, it had taken a whole night for her to arrive. What could Prince Rupert do to her in a night? Sophia didn't want to think about that.

They reached a set of gilded doors that led through to rooms of exquisite opulence beyond. There was none of the restraint or simple comfort found in Sebastian's rooms here. Instead, it seemed that every surface featured expense, from gold leaf on the woodwork to the finest painted porcelain and cut crystal. The finest of clothes were discarded casually for servants to pick up, while other doors obviously led to further rooms.

"So," Rupert said, "my brother has put you aside. Has he tired of you so quickly?"

It was deliberately hurtful.

"Things with Sebastian were complicated," Sophia said.

"They were simple," Rupert replied, moving over to one of a pair of high-backed chairs. "My brother wanted you, and you wanted position at the court, so you only allowed him to bed you in return for a marriage proposal. Then, when he finally came to his senses, Sebastian realized that he couldn't be bound to a noble girl with no lands, no real title, no wealth, and no army. Sit here."

Rupert added the last with a casual jerk of his hand toward the other chair. Sophia went to it, because she doubted that she would be able to make it to the door if she ran. She sat as demurely as she could, but one glance at the prince's thoughts told her it was too little, too late.

"I have learned to be more honest about these things," Rupert said. "You are beautiful, and you have at least some semblance of nobility, so if you are entertaining, I will keep you here for a time. I will do what I want with you, and in return, I will give you gifts that you will no doubt sell discreetly like the whore you are. When I grow bored with you, you will leave, but a reputation as one of my lovers will probably make it easy enough to ply your trade with nobles more of your own rank. It will be a very satisfactory arrangement all around."

Sophia couldn't contain her shock. "You think that I'm some kind of... of *courtesan*?"

Rupert pointed to a spot on the floor. "Kneel there. *Kneel* or I will force you to."

Sophia did as he commanded, but as she did so, she looked around for something she could use as a weapon, or a distraction. Something that would let her get out of this room. There was nothing close to hand, though.

"I think that you are whatever I decide," Rupert said. "I don't mind a little defiance, because it adds spice, but don't forget for an instant the truth of your situation. I can make you do whatever I want. I could tie you to that chair and whip you bloody if I wished it, and nobody would lift a finger to help you. Perhaps I will."

Sophia shivered at the memory of what had happened to her at the House of the Unclaimed. This time, it seemed as though her sister wouldn't be coming to save her. She looked into Prince Rupert's mind, trying to find some lever that she could use to talk her way out of this, some secret or hint of the past that she could manipulate him with. All that yielded, though, was the depths of his cruelty, and all the things he wanted to do to her.

Sophia heard the click of the door and started to look round, but Rupert moved faster than she did, catching her by the hair in a flare of pain that brought tears to her eyes.

"I didn't tell you to move," he said. "Remain where you are."

Sophia did as he bid her, trying to think, hoping for a way out of this. She looked to the servant who came with two glasses of wine on a tray, but the woman wasn't looking at Sophia. She was very carefully not looking, and Sophia could sense her reasons: she didn't want to risk being dismissed for interfering. Worse, she didn't want to risk being pulled into what was going to happen next.

So she placed the wine tray on a side table and left without a word, ignoring the way Sophia knelt there with Rupert's hand still balled in her hair.

"You like this, don't you?" Rupert demanded.

"No," Sophia shot back.

He slapped her. "Liar. All of your sort pretend at being so meek and innocent, but look at you. Wearing a whore's dress. Coming back to my rooms." He took one of the wine glasses and pressed it to Sophia's lips as gently as if his outburst hadn't just happened. "Drink."

Sophia drank, feeling the burn of the wine, tasting its sweetness. She watched Rupert set that glass aside, then pick up the second and drink from it. He kissed her roughly then, holding her in place, the taste of the wine still on his lips.

It was nothing like the kisses she'd had with Sebastian. There was no gentleness to it, only control, no passion, only violence. It was an act of possession rather than anything to do with love, or even real desire. It was simply a way for the prince to declare his power over Sophia, and she knew that there would be worse to come.

"No," Sophia said, pulling back from him. "No."

She reeled as Rupert hit her again, but she didn't care. She pushed away from him, forcing her way to her feet and running for the door. She didn't care then who saw her, or what trouble it might mean for her in the future. She just wanted to get away.

Rupert brought her down before she'd gone half a dozen steps, tackling Sophia around the ankles and then wrapping his arms around her while she cried out. Sophia found her arms grabbed and wrenched up above her head, tied in place with a speed that said that the prince had done this more than once before.

"Did you really think you could get away?" Rupert asked. "Oh, Sophia, I'm not some weakling like my brother. I'm a real prince. A strong prince. One who can take what he wants."

He laughed as he lifted her, carrying her bodily toward one of the rooms connected to the main chamber. Sophia screamed for help, both in the privacy of her mind and more vocally. None of it seemed to make any difference.

When she saw that the room on the other side was a bedroom, Sophia tried to fight. Rupert just laughed at it, carrying her easily and throwing her down onto the bed roughly. Sophia found her bound hands grabbed and tied in place to the wooden frame of it, so that although she could buck and roll, she couldn't pull clear. She could see Rupert watching her while she did it, and his thoughts just fueled her panic.

"I don't know how long you'll last," Rupert said. "But something tells me it will be a while. I like taming wild things. Shall we begin?"

CHAPTER FOURTEEN

Sebastian tried to look like a prince rather than just another seasick soldier as the ship carrying his company cut through the waves of the Knifewater. It wasn't easy, because his stomach threatened to rebel with every lurch of the vessel, but he forced himself to stay strong with the determination not to embarrass himself, his family, or the crown.

Rupert, he suspected, would have made a better job of it. His brother was the dashing one, the brave soldier with the reputation for skill at arms. He had commanded forces, while Sebastian was stuck as a junior officer, just one man among hundreds. He had fought in battles against rebels and mercenaries, enemies abroad and foes at home. He was halfway to being a storybook prince, while Sebastian couldn't even master his own emotions.

Thoughts of Sophia intruded with every instant that passed, reminding Sebastian of just how weak he was. A dutiful prince should have been able to push the need for her aside, blank his mind of everything except the coming conflict. He should have been able to keep from remembering the scent of her skin, the touch of her lips. Instead, Sebastian found himself aching with the memory of her.

He hoped she was safe. Her sister, Kate, had been a terrifying little thing, but at least she had protected Sophia from the worst that Ashton had to offer. Sebastian wished that he had been able to do it; that he hadn't sent her away in the first place, but some things couldn't be changed; they could only be borne.

Like this damnable sea crossing. The distance between the southern shores of his mother's kingdom and the continent beyond might only be a brief one, but this crossing that was supposed to last a few hours already felt as though it had stretched into a lifetime.

"Mind your back, your highness!" a sailor said, a fraction of a second before water sloshed around Sebastian's boots, splashing up as far as his knees. "Sorry!"

Sebastian could have turned angrily, but instead he made himself walk away. He had no doubt that the behavior was deliberate, as so much else had been since he set foot on the ship.

He'd heard the muttered comments of the sailors behind his back, found himself "accidentally" nudged and barged whenever he got in their way. On one occasion, he thought he heard part of the "March of Loroch Aird," with all its anti-monarchical sentiments, being whistled behind his back.

He walked up to the bridge, although in its way, the behavior of the officers had been little better. It had been punctilious, even deferential, but Sebastian had spent enough time at court to know the ways in which even that could be turned into a kind of mockery. There was certainly none of the casual camaraderie he had hoped for, nothing that went beyond formal politeness and into friendship.

He moved up to the spot where General Sir Aubery Lanchster-Courte, commander of this expedition, was making his plans. The general was an older man, plump and jowly, but with decades of experience behind him. Sebastian offered him a salute as he approached. He might be a prince, but the older man commanded.

"Did you want something, your highness?" the general asked. There was no unfriendliness there, but no friendliness either, just a kind of politeness with nothing behind it.

"I was just wondering if you'd noticed anything odd about the behavior of the men," Sebastian asked.

"Nothing at all," the general replied. "Why, have you?"

"Some of the men seem a little… unfriendly," Sebastian said. "I was wondering if perhaps I had done something to offend them. I would hate to think that I'm affecting morale."

The general stood considering him for a moment, and Sebastian thought that perhaps he was about to say something, but he seemed to think better of it.

"I am sure there will be no issue, your highness," he said. "My men are very disciplined. With so many on one ship, a little fractiousness is only to be expected. Now, if you will excuse me, there are still preparations that need to be made."

It was a polite dismissal, but it was still a dismissal. Sebastian found himself another railing to lean against and filled himself with thoughts of Sophia once more. He was still thinking it when he heard a snort beside him.

"You really don't know why they hate you?"

Sebastian turned and found himself looking at a broad-shouldered, fork-bearded man wearing a sergeant's stripes on his tunic.

"Feel free to enlighten me," Sebastian said. "Sergeant…"

"Varkin," the other man said with a shrug. "Let's just say that we've seen our fill of princes."

Sebastian frowned at that. "My brother?" he said. "But Rupert is—"

"I know what he is," the sergeant said. "Do you?"

"But I've heard the stories of the battles he's won," Sebastian said. "He was at Olds Hill."

He saw Varkin nod. "Aye, when he wasn't running away. Sat back and let better men die, and then charged in at the end to take the glory."

Sebastian tried to dredge up other battles that his brother had been involved in. "He's put down rebellions. He's fought a dozen places."

"If you could call it fighting," Varkin replied. "Safe sorties against groups we knew we'd outnumber. Butchering idiot peasants too slow to get out of the way, then calling them an army. Hardly the glory you hear about, is it? Not that I'm complaining. I'll take a safe fight over getting butchered in battle any day. And now here we are, escorting the next in line to build his legend on nothing."

Sebastian wanted to say that it wasn't like that, and that Rupert wasn't like that. The trouble was, he knew his brother. Was it so hard to believe that he would take easy glory slaughtering peasants over a real fight? Even so, he wouldn't be tarred with the same brush.

"We're going to the continent," Sebastian pointed out. "I suspect there will be enough real fights for everyone."

The other man laughed at that, in a big, booming explosion of sound.

"You aren't serious? You *are*, aren't you?" He laughed again. "That's why you've been standing there like you actually believe you're a hero? You think that you're going over to fight all the free companies and the Disestablishers, the guild armies and the imperialists? You probably think that you're going to take on the New Army by yourself."

As if the first few weren't wars worth fighting, and the last was impossible. Now, Sebastian had to admit that he was getting a little annoyed. "You think I can't fight?"

"Of course you can't fight!" the other man said. "That's why we're heading to one of the Strait Islands with hundreds of men to put down a few dozen peasants who have decided to declare a free kingdom, as far away from the real war as we can get."

Sebastian shook his head. "No, there must be some mistake."

"No mistake," Varkin said. "Do you think I'd sign up for this if there were a real chance of getting killed? We're going to go to Least Isle and remind a few farmers of the price of rebellion."

He said it as though it was a joke, but Sebastian couldn't see the funny side of it. Was this really what this was about? Sending him away to a non-battle to build his reputation? The worst part was that it sounded far too much like the kind of thing his mother might do.

Sebastian stood there, looking out, and tried to hide his disappointment.

***

When the island came into view, it was even smaller than Sebastian had suspected it would be. Just a few miles across, with scrub and grass, but more rocks than either. It was the kind of place that barely seemed big enough to warrant settling, let alone fighting over.

Even so, the far side of the island was out of sight around a spur of rock that jutted out into the water like the reaching branch of a tree. Perhaps there was more to it.

"Will we be sending scouts first?" Sebastian asked General Lanchster-Courte.

"And risk giving away the fact that we're here?" the general replied. "Let's not pretend that we're walking into real danger here. It's a few farmers. We have an entire company. We will advance as one and get this over with. Bosun, take us in close. It's not as if this rabble will have the artillery to target us."

"But General—" Sebastian began.

"Your highness," the general said, cutting him off, "I am a man who does his duty, even if it means participating in this farce. But I will not stand here and be told how to do that duty by a man who has his rank because of his birth rather than because of any knowledge or skill. We will proceed to the landing boats and take this island. You will stay beside me and not even *attempt* to do something so foolish as issue orders. Do otherwise, and I will confine you to your cabin until this is over."

They were the sternest words Sebastian had heard from anyone but his mother in a long time, and for the moment, they were enough to render him speechless. He fell into step beside the general, following him to one of the many landing boats, where soldiers were already waiting with a mixture of swords and axes, crossbows and clumsy-looking muskets. Some wore hints of armor, but most didn't.

For his part, Sebastian wore a breastplate and gauntlets, but not the kind of full armor that might have been used for ceremonies. He had his sword at his hip, along with a dagger and a pistol whose powder he hoped would remain dry on the journey across, although it didn't seem likely.

They rowed, although no one seemed to expect Sebastian to play a part in it. Indeed, it seemed that none of them really cared whether he was there or not. When they splashed up onto the beach, no one moved to help him. Sebastian had to scramble out on his own, the weight of his partial armor making the whole process take twice as long as it should in the water.

They moved up the beach in a great mass of men, although Sebastian noted that he and the general were toward the back. He suspected that the idea was to protect him even from the few fragments of danger that there were on the island, and he knew better than to argue.

A man called as he found a route up off the beach, and quickly, the soldiers started on their way. Three hundred of them at least, well armed, and more than enough to deal with an island rabble, yet still Sebastian could feel a sense of wrongness running through him. The island seemed too quiet, too still.

"General, there's something wrong," he said.

"If you are going to add cowardice to uselessness, I will send you back to the ship," the general said, and something about his tone said that he was serious.

"Can't you hear it?" Sebastian insisted.

"I can't hear anything," the general replied.

"That's my point. Why is it so quiet?"

He hadn't been involved in a war before, but Sebastian had been dragged off hunting by his family enough times. Normally, the forests and the fields were full of the sound of birdsong or the movement of small animals. The only time it grew quiet was when things were hiding, waiting.

"General—" Sebastian began.

"I've had enough of this," the general replied. "Your talking is enough to wake the—"

Noise ripped across the beach, in the deep boom of cannon fire. Sebastian saw splinters fly from their ship as cannonballs struck it, and he cursed the fact that they'd come in so close, not believing that their foes could ever have real weapons.

Next to those deep booms, the crackle of musket fire was quieter, but only just. Sebastian saw the general clutch his chest and fall, while a dozen other men went down in that first volley. For a moment, he stood there, not knowing what was going on, and it was clear that the others there were the same.

Men advanced along the beach in tight formation. These weren't farmers or rebellious islanders. Instead, they wore ochre tunics and carried pikes, bows, and muskets in equal measure. Sebastian knew enough about the affairs of the continent to recognize the uniform of the New Army when he saw it.

"Ambush!" he yelled, but it was already too late for it. Men were already dying around him, brought down by shot or bolts, not even having a chance to make it up past the beach. Out on the water, the ship that had brought them was starting to list, holed near the waterline and already sinking.

Sebastian saw what must have happened. That the New Army must have advanced more than they thought, taking the islands in the middle of the uprising. It meant... it meant a lot of things. That they'd thought they were coming for a fight that would be little more than a slaughter, only to face a real force. That the men in front of them wouldn't run, only try to kill.

Above all, it meant that Sebastian had gotten his wish. He was facing a real fight.

Now he just had to survive it.

CHAPTER FIFTEEN

In her chains, Kate dreamed, and the dream was a familiar one. Ashton lay beneath her, and in it, people died. They screamed as men in ochre tunics moved through the streets, killing and looting with no sense of restraint or remorse. They slaughtered the people, and there was nothing anyone could do about it.

She was running through the streets now, running away from the oncoming soldiers. Kate turned and there was a blade in her hand. She struck out with it, feeling it glide through flesh as easily as water. She turned and ran again, off into the shadows, always moving.

She was running through the forest now, but somehow that forest sat within the walls of the home that always haunted her dreams. Trees grew out of the walls, their branches burning as the fire started to claim them. Flowers and briars grew up to form the frames of paintings, and now those paintings held a mixture of long dead ancestors and people Kate had killed. There were the veiled faces of the masked sisters, the rough visages of soldiers, the younger features of the boy she'd killed on the road, what felt like a lifetime ago.

Siobhan was there, or a dream version of her at least, more plant than woman, more wild spirit than either. She sat in the middle of a banqueting hall, on the lip of a fountain that was somehow in the center of the floor, masked figures dancing around it. She dipped a cup into the fountain, offering it to dancer after dancer.

It was only as Kate moved closer that she saw that the fountain didn't run with water now, but blood.

The dancers consumed it happily, sipping it like the finest wine or quaffing it like beer. They laughed as they danced, even when their dancing turned to spasms and they started to fall, dying as they hit the floor.

Siobhan seemed to laugh loudest of all, and there was nothing human in that laughter, nothing peaceful or quiet. It wasn't the laugh of something evil, just something so alien to human thought that it might amount to the same thing and never notice. When the dream Siobhan turned to Kate, Kate found herself drawn forward, taking a cup of the poisonous blood without even hesitating. She lifted it to her lips…

…and woke, gasping for breath. She lay there for long seconds in the tent they'd put her in, guards surrounding it as if worried that she might try to escape at any moment. Perhaps she would have, if not for the heavy chains holding her. Escaping them was one thing that Siobhan's lessons hadn't covered.

Siobhan. Kate didn't know what her dream meant, if it meant anything at all. She actually felt a little guilty about the content of her latest nightmare. She was the forest woman's apprentice, so shouldn't she trust her more than that? It seemed though that some deep part of her had its fears about her new teacher, and Kate couldn't honestly say that there was no reason for them.

She pushed that thought aside, considering her captivity. Should she call for help with her powers, to either Siobhan or Sophia? Sophia would be more likely to come, but it was hard to see what she might be able to do. Of the two of them, Kate was the strong one, and if she couldn't break free on her own, it was hard to see what her sister might do.

Kate was still thinking about calling for help when she heard the sounds of an argument growing outside.

"And *I* say that you can't go in there. This is the camp of Lord Cranston's company, not some city street."

"Street or not, we are still in the Dowager's domain. Stand aside. You've a murderer in there!"

Kate knew that they were talking about her. She could sense plenty of minds around her, enough that she would have had no chance of slipping past them, even if she hadn't been chained. She caught the thoughts of men approaching, and a moment later found herself blinking in the sunlight as it streamed in through the tent flap.

"Up you!" a man bellowed. He looked more like a watchman than a soldier, with a club in place of a sword, and manacles at his belt. Another like him followed behind, and they grabbed Kate by the arms when she didn't move.

How could she kill so many? the one who'd come in first thought.

She didn't make it easy for them to lift her. She didn't struggle, exactly, but Kate saw no reason to make an effort. She forced the watchmen to lift her weight, all but carrying her from the tent.

Outside, she saw something that looked as though it might be the start of a battle. There were soldiers lined up now, blocking the road back to Ashton, while half a dozen watchmen stood before them, accompanied by a masked priest who pointed at Kate as soon as he saw her. Will was there too, although there were soldiers in his way, obviously there to prevent him from interfering, or even talking to her. She just hoped that they hadn't hurt him because of her.

"That's the one!" the priest said, and Kate could hear the fear in his voice. "She came to the House of the Unclaimed and she murdered men, women, and children!"

"That's not true!" Kate snapped back, and it wasn't. She hadn't touched any of the orphans there, just their tormentors. The distinction might be a fine one to anyone else, but to her, it was the only one that mattered. She had given them what they deserved.

The soldiers around her ignored her, but they did move in on the watchmen, silently and stoically. Right then, Kate felt as though she didn't matter to them so much as this intrusion onto their territory did.

"This is our prisoner," one of them said. "We're holding her until Lord Cranston arrives to decide what to do with her."

"We are representatives of the *law*," one of the watchmen snapped back, but he let go of Kate's arm. Briefly, she considered running, but Kate doubted she would get a dozen steps without being cut down. The soldiers were only keeping her there for their commander's judgment, after all.

"And we're the ones who make sure there's enough of a country for there to be a law in," the soldier shot back.

"You? Mercenaries who fight for the highest bidder?"

Kate could sense the tension rising now. It was obvious that the men disliked one another, resentments rising to the surface that had nothing to do with her. In the fragments of thoughts that she caught around her, she found hints of old scores and older resentments, of mercenaries who came into the city with too much money and fists that were too ready to fight, of watchmen who would never be real soldiers, but who insisted on harassing those who were.

"That girl is a murderer!" the priest repeated, pointing at Kate once more as if the identification hadn't been clear enough the first time. "A murderer, a runaway, a thief, and more."

"All of that?" the soldier asked. "Well for us, she came here and beat our men in the training ring, then killed our sword master and half a dozen other men besides."

"All the more reason to hand her over to hang," the priest insisted.

Kate had the feeling that she might as well not have been there. They barely looked at her as they argued, bickering more because of who they were than because of what she'd done. She found herself half hoping that they fell to fighting one another, because if that happened, she might have a chance of escaping in the confusion. Will was the only one who looked her way, and he was in no position to help.

"We have our orders," the soldier said. "You think some of us don't want to kill her here and now, get it over with?" He did shoot a glance Kate's way then, so full of venom that she took a step back automatically. One of the watchmen caught her arm.

"We have the right to her," he said.

"And *we* have orders to hold her until Lord Cranston arrives," the soldier shot back, grabbing for Kate's other arm. "By force, if necessary."

For a moment, Kate suspected that she might be about to be pulled in half like some frayed rope in a tug of war. The two men jerked at her arms, and it was only the fact that there were still guards there, ready to fire on her if she ran, that kept her from throwing them both from their feet.

They were still pulling at her when Kate saw the rider. He was approaching at a brisk trot, a feathered hat shading him from the sun. He wore a uniform that had probably been a fine gold once, but now looked almost gray with wear and sun damage. Despite that, he sat tall in the saddle, one hand resting on the hilt of a duelist's sword, just a little way from one of a pair of matched pistols. As he rode closer, Kate could see that he was at least forty, with an oiled beard that was nevertheless running to gray.

None of that impressed her. What did was the way the soldiers around Kate responded to his approach. The ones on the road parted as smoothly as corn before a scythe, standing erect, their weapons held up in a kind of salute. Every man there watched him as though waiting for something to happen, taut as a bowstring with the readiness to answer any order. They seemed utterly in awe of him.

Kate had seen plenty of people who had been able to inspire obedience through fear, and a few who had managed to do it through others' faith. She'd felt the power that Siobhan had. This was something different. There was respect, real respect there, shading into something close to admiration among the older soldiers. It was enough to catch her interest, even if fear rose at the same time that this would be the man who condemned her.

Of course, none of the watchmen there so much as noticed him until he was almost level with them. The priest, in particular, was so busy staring at Kate with hatred that when the newcomer rode up next to him, the man practically jumped in shock.

"What is going on here?" the newcomer said. "I received a message about a fight in my company, yet I get here and I find half of it guarding one girl, while the rest are surrounding the watch." He turned to the priest. "Who might you be, sir?"

"I am Kirkus, priest of the Masked Goddess and second secretary to the high priestess *herself*. I demand that you hand over that girl!"

"Oh, you demand, do you?" the newcomer said. Kate knew instantly that it had been the wrong way to put it. He dismounted with a certain stiffness. "I am Lord Peter Cranston, and you will be silent until I require more of you. Jerrel, you're a sensible man. Report, please. What is all this about?"

"The girl came to our camp before with the recruit Will, sir," an older soldier said, stepping forward. He gave a salute so crisp he practically vibrated with it. "She demanded to fight and was beaten on the orders of sword master Evans. She came back while we were practicing with the recruit—"

"Practicing, or punishing?"

The soldier hesitated only a moment. "Punishing, sir. The sword master wanted an example made."

"An example of his stupidity, perhaps," Lord Cranston said. "What then?"

"She cut Evans to pieces, sir, along with half a dozen other men. She was faster than I could see for some of it, although my eyes aren't what they were, I'll admit."

The older man looked thoughtful. Finally, he did the one thing that none of the others had bothered with. He turned his attention to Kate.

"Is all of that true?" Lord Cranston asked, and there was something about the sharp lines of his face that warned Kate not to lie. This was a man who'd spent enough time around liars to know the difference.

"Yes," she said. She could have injected remorse into her tone, but that would have been another kind of lie.

"You tried to join our company? Why?"

Kate shrugged. "I wanted to learn to fight. I thought it would be a good life."

"Even though young women don't usually join the free companies?"

Kate didn't flinch under his gaze. "I don't have much time for what's usual."

Lord Cranston nodded, then, snake fast, he struck at Kate. She reacted on reflex, catching his arm in midair, despite her chains. He nodded thoughtfully.

"Good enough," he said. He turned back to the others. "You, priest, Kirkus or whatever your name is. What is your complaint?"

"My complaint?" the priest said. "My *complaint* is that this girl murdered priests and priestesses, set light to the city's House of the Unclaimed, and released half of our charges into the streets."

Lord Cranston turned back to Kate, raising one bushy eyebrow. "Is that part true?"

Kate nodded. How could she expect this man to understand what she'd been through, or the reasons for it all? "They beat my sister senseless and sold her to a slaver. I'd have burnt it years ago if I could."

The nobleman stood there, and Kate knew that he couldn't understand, yet a look at his thoughts said that he did. There were thoughts there of a childhood where the whip had never been far away, and of blood spilled in a long life.

"Yes," he said, "I imagine you would." He turned to the priest. "I'm sorry, priest, but this is clearly a case where military law must take precedence."

"But you have no right!" the priest complained, and the watchmen gathered around him as if they might try to drag Kate away by force. She saw some of the soldiers shift; not much, but enough.

Lord Cranston stopped them with the barest movement of his hand.

"How familiar are you with the laws of the land, priest?" he asked.

"I know all of—"

"Good," Lord Cranston said. "Then you will be familiar with the right of authorized companies to take on criminals as part of their sentence?"

Kate wasn't sure that she'd heard that right. She was expecting to be told how she would die, and now... now it sounded as though she was being offered a position in the company. She saw the priest redden at that.

"But you can't—"

"I can, and I am," Lord Cranston said. "Because I have what is known in military circles as *more men than you*. Are you familiar with the concept?"

Now, the red of the priest's complexion turned an angry white. Kate couldn't blame him. She could barely overcome her own shock.

"The high priestess will hear of this."

"Tell the Dowager herself," Lord Cranston said. "But I doubt that she will object to it. This girl can fight well enough to down half a dozen of my men. She beat my sword master, and although he was a vile man, he could fight. There is war coming, and not just the petty wars that have filled the continent for a hundred years. This New Army they talk about is sweeping away all who stand before them, and killing anyone who tries to stand for anything. In the face of that, I will take anyone I can get. Someone like her is a definite improvement on farmers who barely know which end of a sword to hold. Now go, please, before I show you which it is."

The priest looked as though he might say something, but one of the watchmen caught his arm, pulling him back.

"You haven't heard the last of this," he called.

"You know," Lord Cranston said, "I rather think I have. Now, Jerrel, get these chains off her, would you? It makes it look as though our whole company is afraid of one girl."

The old soldier cocked his head to one side. "Most of us are, sir."

He went to do it anyway, loosening the shackles. Kate shook them off, rubbing her wrists. She looked over to Will, who looked just as stunned as she felt by all this.

"What now?" she asked.

"What now, *sir*!" the old soldier, Jerrel, corrected her.

"That's all right, Jerrel," Lord Cranston said. "I'm sure she'll get the hang of it. What's your name, girl?"

"Kate… sir," Kate said.

"Well, I'm Lord Cranston. You can call me that, or 'my lord' or 'sir.' I really don't care which. Do you still want to join my company?"

Kate considered the alternatives. It didn't take long.

"Yes, my lord."

"Evans was right about one thing: we can't have a girl as a raw recruit. Luckily, I have a need of a bagman. You will stay by me, follow my orders, run my errands, and learn whatever I wish to teach you of the arts of war. Is that understood?"

It was brusque, but Kate could sense a certain friendliness behind it all.

"Yes, my lord," she said.

"Good," Lord Cranston said. "And let's hope that you're as good with a blade as the men claim. War is coming."

Kate knew that.

She'd *seen* it.

CHAPTER SIXTEEN

Sophia fought to get free of Rupert's bed as he approached her, but tied as she was, she could barely move, let alone run away. There was no mercy in his eyes, no sense that he might change his mind about what he was going to do, or realize the full horror of it.

He stripped off his shirt with the kind of languor that in Sebastian might have been sensual, but Sophia could see his thoughts, and she knew that he was merely taking his time, enjoying her helplessness. In another man, the muscled torso he revealed might have been an object of desire, but here, it was only a sign that Sophia was one step closer to the moment when he would do all the things that for now were only contained in his thoughts.

He was imagining what he would do as he moved closer. Sophia did her best to shut it out, but even so, the thoughts mingled with the reality until Sophia wasn't sure which was which. Rupert moved closer to her still, kneeling on the bed beside her and reaching for her in a delicate parody of tenderness.

"No," Sophia begged as he touched her face. "Please."

His hand went to her throat, tightening just enough that Sophia couldn't beg.

"We've been through this," Rupert said. "Whores don't get to say no to their betters."

He forced another kiss on her then, his mouth hungry and brutal in equal measure. His hands moved over Sophia, seeking out the stays of her dress, undoing them one by one. When she moaned in complaint, he reared up over her.

"You see, I knew you'd enjoy it if only you tried."

Sophia didn't reply. She knew there was nothing she could say, nothing she could do, that would change his mind or stop what was to come. She shut her eyes against it instead, determined to give her tormentor no satisfaction, to pretend that she was no more than a dead thing in the face of his assault.

Distantly, Sophia heard the click of a door.

"No, that won't do," Rupert said above her, and slapped her, bringing Sophia's eyes open with a jerk. "I want to see those pretty eyes. I want to see the hatred there, and the moment when it turns into obedience."

Sophia wasn't looking at him then, though. She was looking past him, to where a figure in one of the indentureds' plain clothes crept forward on silent feet. Sophia recognized Cora, the servant who had helped her to disguise what she was. Her heart swelled as she picked up one of the gilded statuettes that decorated the room, weighing it in her hand.

"What are you staring at?" Rupert demanded.

Too late, Sophia realized that she was giving away Cora's presence with her staring. She tried to look up at Rupert, tried to give him what he wanted, but it was too late. He was already turning.

"Who in all the hells are you?" Rupert demanded. "No matter. You just earned yourself—"

Sophia didn't get to hear the rest of his threat, because in that moment, Cora hit him with the statuette, and Sophia felt a moment of almost complete satisfaction as it struck Rupert just above the temple, the thud of it audible around the room.

The prince staggered for a moment and then fell off the bed, facedown on the floor. He didn't move.

"Oh, goddess," Cora said. "I think I've killed him. I had to hit him. I had to help you, but... I've killed him!"

"You haven't killed him," Sophia said, although right then she would have been happy if Cora had. "Look, he's still breathing."

"He's still breathing," Cora said, her breath coming fast. "He's still breathing."

Sophia suspected that she should have been the one panicking, but right then she just felt numb. She felt empty with all the things she'd seen in Rupert's thoughts. All the things that he'd been planning for her. He might not have had a chance to do them, but even so, the images wouldn't go away.

"Untie me," Sophia said. "Cora, you need to untie me. Focus."

"Yes, yes, of course," Cora said. She let the statuette fall to the floor and went to Sophia, working at the knots that held her. "They're going to execute me. I hit a prince with a statue!"

"To save me," Sophia reminded Cora as she rubbed feeling back into her wrists. She tried to stand and almost fell, but managed to find her footing. With fumbling fingers, she started to refasten the stays of her dress. She couldn't get them because she was shaking too much now as the full horror of what had just happened seeped into her.

"It won't matter to them," Cora said. She fastened the stays where Sophia couldn't, helping her toward the door. "Assaulting a prince is treason and I... I'm not even free. It would be the lead mask for me, or the breaking wheel."

"For us," Sophia said, because it was the truth. There was no way that Rupert would let her live now. At best, she would find herself hanged or beheaded. At worst... at worst, he might decide to do it himself in ways that were too horrific to contemplate.

A part of her wanted to go back as she thought that. She wanted to go back and hit Rupert with the statuette again and again until there was nothing left but a stain on the floor. She wanted to kill him, both for what he'd tried to do and what he might do in the future. Only the thought of Sebastian stopped her. How would she feel if she'd been told that he'd killed Kate?

No, she couldn't do it.

"We need to get out of here," Sophia said. She caught Cora by the arm. "Come on, Cora. You can't stay here now. We need to walk out of here, and we need to pretend that everything is normal."

"I don't know if I can do that," Cora said.

"You can," Sophia said, forcing herself to sound more confident than she felt. She felt like an empty shell then, but if she let Cora see that, she suspected that the other woman would fall apart. "It's easy to pretend. I managed to be a noblewoman for weeks. You can pretend that you're okay for a few minutes."

She pulled Cora toward the door, then out into the corridors of the palace. They moved slowly, because right then, Sophia wasn't sure she was steady enough to do more, and because the last thing they needed to do was run. If they ran, guards would stop them, wanting to know why, and Sophia suspected that they would see the guilt written on their faces in an instant.

So they walked, as quickly as they could manage, leaning on one another for support. The corridors seemed to stretch out forever, so that Sophia was sure that they would never make it from the palace before Rupert woke up and called for help.

If he woke up. Would Sophia feel bad if the man who'd just tried to rape her died? For him, not for an instant. She would even be happy knowing that no other girl would ever suffer through what she'd just suffered. Even so, she would feel bad for Sebastian, who would feel the pain of losing a brother. Then there was what would happen to her if Rupert died.

They would never stop hunting her.

Sophia pushed that thought away, continuing to walk with Cora. Servants glanced at them, but said nothing and made no move toward them. Sophia doubted that she and Cora were truly acting well enough for things to appear normal, so why didn't they intervene?

She knew the answer to that at once: they were used to seeing young women staggering from Prince Rupert's rooms, looking haunted and shaken. They'd seen it before, and they'd learned from experience that it was better not to get involved.

Sophia found herself hoping that Rupert died again.

"What are you still doing here?"

Sophia turned to see Milady d'Angelica approaching down one of the corridors. Sophia did her best to ignore her. There was no time for this.

"I told you before," Angelica said, "if you didn't leave I would have you dragged out. Did you think I was joking?"

Sophia turned toward her. "Right now, I don't care if you live or die," she said. "But if you don't turn and walk away, I swear I'll kill you."

Angelica raised her hands, stepping back in obvious shock from the sheer venom of it. Perhaps that would have been an end to it if that hadn't been the moment when voices sounded behind Sophia, demanding answers and action at a volume that could only mean one thing: they'd found Rupert.

Angelica stared at the two of them for a moment, seeming to realize what was happening. A slow, vicious smile spread over her face.

"They're here!" Angelica called out. "Guards! This way!"

Sophia shoved her back, enjoying the sensation of sending her sprawling. Then she grabbed Cora's arm and ran.

"Which way?" she demanded, not slowing down for an instant. "Cora, you know the palace. Which way out?"

"There's a servant's entrance," Cora said. "This way."

They ran, and behind them, Sophia could hear shouts now. She ran ahead of them, and only spotted a cluster of minds ahead of her, jerking Cora to the side just as guards burst from a side room.

They ran on, heading into a kitchen space filled with heat and noise and bustling work. Sophia and Cora pushed their way past cooks and kitchen helpers, ignoring the shouts of outrage as pots clattered from work surfaces and spit dogs ran around yapping. Sophia dared a glance over her shoulder; there were guards there, pushing their way through it all, slowed only slightly by the chaos Sophia and Cora had caused.

There was a door ahead of them, bound in iron. They ran for it, and Sophia was relieved to find it unlocked. She threw it open and then ran out with Cora in her wake, hurrying through a kitchen garden planted with thyme and sage, vegetables and fruit trees. Sophia dodged through them, all too aware of the risk that the guards might give up chasing and simply shoot after them with lead shot or arrows.

"This way," Cora said, pointing to a set of small side steps.

Sophia ran with her down them, to a door that opened onto the city's streets. The two of them sprinted out across the cobbles, ignoring the shouts of the guard who stood by the small gate, obviously there to keep intruders out and caught completely by surprise by people running from the palace.

He quickly joined the others in running after them, and now Sophia could feel her lungs burning with the effort of running from them all. She chose streets at random, twisting and turning as the pursuers followed them, joined now by some of the people of the city eager to help bring them down from some sense of justice, or because they suspected that there would be a reward.

Kate, Sophia called, *help, please help!*

She sent it more in hope than in any expectation that her sister would hear. She threw the plea out as widely as she could, hoping that she could make Kate hear through sheer volume.

And then what? If she wasn't there, she wouldn't be able to help. Even if she was, could she really hope to fight off the guards who were following? This was Sophia's problem to solve, and right now, the only way she could think of to deal with it was to keep running.

She did, dragging Cora with her, heading from the richer parts of the city into the tangled snarls of small alleys that marked the poor quarters. They ran through lines of laundry hung across streets and jumped over fences. None of it seemed to slow their pursuers.

"I don't know how much longer I can keep running," Cora said.

"If we stop, we die," Sophia shot back. It was as simple as that. Given the anger of the shouts behind them, she wasn't even sure if the royal guards would bother with dragging her back for a trial. They would probably just kill her where she stood, whatever the pretense of a system of laws and judgment.

Sophia ran on, and now the streets opened out. That wasn't a good thing. She and Cora couldn't hope to outrun the guards on a flat stretch. Only the obstacles and twists of the alleys had stopped them from being caught so far.

Quick, a voice said, sounding in her head. *This way.*

A girl stood on the opposite side of the street, next to a cart stacked high with boxes and barrels. She was blonde-haired and her blue dress was streaked with dirt. She was waving to Sophia, and Sophia knew that she was the one who had sent the message.

"This way," she called, out loud this time. "Quick, into the barrels. They won't look there. The merchant is away, so he'll never know."

That was enough for Sophia. She ran over, pulling herself up. The barrels were huge, and most were filled with the strong scent of beer. Sophia knew that there was no choice.

"Inside, Cora," she said. "Quickly."

She leapt into one of the barrels, and the girl pushed the lid down.

Immediately, Sophia couldn't breathe. She'd thought that there might be enough space between the liquid and the top for her to keep her head above the ale, but now she found herself beneath it. She crouched there in the dark of the barrel, her lungs painful with the need for air, and it was all she could do to keep from pushing the lid off.

Then the lid did come off, and Sophia had to fight against the urge to surface as faces peered down into the dark beer.

Just a little longer, the girl sent. "There," she said to figures above, "I told you. Nothing but empty barrels. Now, you should hurry. They're probably getting away."

The space above the barrels cleared, and still, Sophia forced herself to wait.

There, they're gone.

Sophia burst from the barrel, gasping for air. The street around her wasn't empty, but there were no guards there now, only the usual people of the city. She'd done it. She'd escaped.

Who are you? Sophia sent to the girl who stood there by the cart.

My name is Emeline. I know your sister. And a friend of hers is a friend of mine.

CHAPTER SEVENTEEN

Around Sebastian, men died, and there was nothing he could do to stop it. They died as musket balls and arrows struck them. They died as the New Army's men charged in with swords and pikes. The sand around him turned to a bloodstained mess, and there was no sign of its cessation.

Sebastian saw a man fall as an arrow struck him through the chest, another cut down by the sweep of a sword, and then there was no time to think, because the rush of men reached him.

He drew his sword and shoved aside a pike, getting in close to strike back at an opponent and feeling the blade sink in. There was very little art to it this close, just a frantic stab and the hope that it would be enough. His opponent's eyes widened as he struck, and the man fell.

Another stepped forward quickly, and Sebastian had to parry, giving ground. He struck out at a foe who was tangled in grappling with one of the sailors who had come with him, striking the man in the leg. He reared back, and that gave the sailor enough room to kill him with a knife.

The battle had been going a matter of moments, but already, Sebastian felt exhausted with it. It felt as though he'd been fighting for a lifetime. He ducked under the swing of a pike, parried another, and gave ground again. Around Sebastian, men milled in confusion, fighting for their lives, with no orders to follow.

The general's body lay on the sand, still against the gold of it. Sebastian knew that there would be no orders coming from there. The general had ordered him not to risk giving commands, but now, who else was there? Sebastian had no way of knowing which officers still lived and which had been brought down by the brutal volleys of projectiles.

As if in answer to that thought, there was another roar of cannon, the shots slamming into their already stricken ship to bring it down quicker. Musket fire struck more of his men, and Sebastian knew he had to act before they were cut to pieces.

"Into the shelter of the cliffs!" he yelled. "All of you. They can't fire at you if they can't see you!"

He pulled back, hoping that the move would draw the others with him. Some men stood where they were, unwilling to take his orders. More went with him, his royal status giving him enough authority to carry them with him. They pulled back from the pikes and the swords, heading for a spot where cliff walls gave them at least some cover, and rocks started to break up the ground.

"Stay together," Sebastian ordered. "I want an orderly withdrawal, not a rout! We can hold them together. Stand, damn you!"

He bellowed it, because it was the only way to be heard above the noise of the battlefield. The men around him looked shocked by the force of it, but they stood. They stood, and they fought.

There was nothing elegant about the violence of the battle. Sebastian had seen duels on the walkways of gardens or in the long viewing galleries of houses. Those had always been displays of speed and bravery, skill and style. This was survival pure and simple.

Sebastian hacked at a man who came at him with a sword, then shoved another who was about to skewer the man standing next to him. He felt the pain of a blade sliding across his cheek, but the kiss of it was barely a glance, and Sebastian killed the man who'd struck at him in return. Around him, men fought and killed and died, again and again, in a cycle that seemed to have no end to it.

Then, suddenly, there *was* an end, as the men attacking them fell back, scurrying across the beach at the sound of trumpets with their pikes still set in case Sebastian's men decided to attack.

"They're retreating," a man close to Sebastian said. Sebastian could hear the relief in his voice, but it was a false thing.

Sebastian shook his head. "They're regrouping."

"Aye, they are," a voice said, and Sebastian saw Sergeant Varkin step forward. He was bloodied, but still stood with an axe in his hands as though he might hack his way through the oncoming forces. He looked at Sebastian with something like respect now. "Good job back there, sir. If the general had listened to your warning…"

Sebastian shook his head. There was no time for thinking about what might have been. They needed to think about what might be coming next.

"Take positions among the rocks," he said. "Load your weapons."

Almost to his surprise, the men there obeyed without hesitation, readying muskets and blunderbusses, hefting swords, or just trying to find a safe spot among the rocks.

"Looks like they're your lads now, sir," Varkin said. "You saved them. You saved *us*."

"Not yet," Sebastian said, "but I'm working on it."

For his part, Sebastian took out his pistol, loading a ball and checking the flint.

He was barely in time, as a fresh wave of enemies moved forward, bristling like a hedgehog with pikes as they marched. A few of the enemy fired on them there, forcing Sebastian to duck down behind a rock as stone chips flew.

"Wait for it," Sebastian said, as a couple of men rose up in preparation to fire back. "Don't waste it. Now!"

He rose up from behind the rocks with the others to deliver a volley of fire that ripped into the advancing enemies. He watched as their entire front rank seemed to disappear, brought down by a hail of balls and crossbow bolts.

"Do we charge?" one of the men asked.

Sebastian shook his head. "Hold your ground. Hold!"

They held, and Sebastian felt as though he was holding them in place by force of will. The enemy gathered momentum, moving into a run as they headed for the rocks. Sebastian prepared his sword and waited for them to break on those stony defenses like a tide.

They struck the rocks, and for a moment, everything was chaos. Men rose above the rocks, seeming to blot out the light, and Sebastian thrust and cut, simply hoping to push them back. He treated the stones the way someone from another age might have treated a castle wall pushing back foes as they tried to scramble past, cutting and killing.

Around him, the other men fought with the kind of savagery that only came from being cornered. Sebastian saw a man stuck through by a pike, only to push forward to stab the attacker. He saw Varkin hacking about him with his axe, and another man frantically reloading, firing a blunderbuss so close to an opponent that the sound was deafening.

Most of the others worked with blades or clubs, knowing that there was no time to work with powder and rammers in the face of the assault. Sebastian kept cutting with his sword, slicing into whatever target he could find with no time or space for feints or complex binds. He fought until there was no one left to fight, the assault ebbing again like another wave of a rising tide.

The trouble was that the tide *was* rising, and eventually it would wash over them all. Sebastian had no way of knowing how many ochre-clad soldiers there were on the island, but he doubted that it was just the couple of hundred he'd been sent with to put down the islanders.

"They'll be coming again, sir," Varkin said, and Sebastian noted the honorific. Not "Your highness," but "sir," as if somewhere in all of this Sebastian had proven himself worthy of being called an officer. Sebastian wasn't so sure. He still had to get them out of this alive.

Out of this. Those words stuck in Sebastian's mind. There was only one way to survive this, and it was a desperate one.

"We need to get back to the boats," he said, gesturing to the spot where the landing boats lay on the edge of the beach. The path to them lay invitingly clear, because the bulk of the enemy's forces were busy marshalling for the next attack. There were too many now, and their numbers were growing by the second.

"And leave the cover of the rocks?" a man said.

"If we stay here, we'll be crushed eventually," Sebastian insisted. "If we make for the boats, we at least have a chance."

"A chance of what?" another man demanded. "The ship is gone."

"We still have arms and oars, don't we?" Sebastian shot back. "Men have swum the Knifewater before; we've all heard the stories."

"Aye," one man muttered, "of men who drowned because they listened."

"Of men eaten by tooth-whales and hook squid," another put in.

Sebastian could see their terror, and he knew just how dangerous a stretch of water the Knifewater could be. It had earned its name in the storms that had ripped ships to pieces, the creatures that lurked in its depths. He wasn't going to give up that easily, though, and it seemed that he'd made at least one ally.

"Drown?" Varkin said. "We've got boats, lads! Not drowning is what they're *for*. Now load up again. This is going to get hectic once it starts."

That was one way of putting it. Sebastian guessed that the moment the men made a break for the boats, the main body of the enemy troops would attack them. At the same time, they would be in full view of any weaponry the enemies waiting on the cliffs chose to bring to bear. It would be a desperate gamble, but even that was better than the cold certainty that came with staying there.

Maybe he would live long enough to see Sophia again.

"We'll need two groups," Sebastian said. "One to hold the main body long enough for the other to get the boats into the water. I'll head the first group. Varkin, you command the second."

"With respect, sir, that's a stupid idea. A commander doesn't put himself in danger, and you've already proved yourself too valuable for that."

Sebastian shrugged. "I'm going to. I don't know enough about boats to refloat the landing craft, and I won't ask men to hold on that beach if I'm not there."

He gathered them together, splitting them. The group to go with him got whatever muskets and pistols there were to go around, because they were the group who would need them most. Sebastian ended up with two pistols and a heavy musket in addition to his sword. Perhaps half of the remaining soldiers stood with him, and now they seemed pitifully few compared to the couple of hundred who had swarmed onto the beach, ready to take the island. Sebastian just hoped that they would be enough, as they looked to him as if expecting that he would have all the answers to keep them safe.

"Ready?" he asked the men. There was a dull chorus of assent that said they all understood the dangers in what they were about to do. "Then let's go. Forward!"

Sebastian stepped forward onto the beach, and the men went with him. The ones who'd been assigned to the boats sprinted for them, while he and the others moved forward to intercept the bulk of the enemy forces as they wheeled to halt the escape.

He lifted his borrowed musket to his shoulder, cocked the flint back in its hammer, and fired. Ahead, a man went down, but there were more. There were so many more.

The battlefield exploded into renewed violence. Shots sounded from the cliffs above, and sand sprayed where they struck it. Where they struck men, there was blood, instead. Sebastian forced himself to reload his musket methodically, because the advancing enemies were still far off enough for it to be possible. He raised it again, and saw an officer with gold braid decorating his uniform fall.

Now, there was no time, because the enemy soldiers were pressing in close. Sebastian drew his sword in one hand and a pistol in the other, cutting a man down and then firing at another at close range. He used the barrel to block the incoming sweep of a sword, then struck out again with his own blade.

Around him, men fought for their lives, and the lives of the others trying to get the boats back into the water. Somewhere above

Sebastian, a cannon sounded, and water sprayed as the ball struck it just beyond the small landing craft.

Varkin's voice bellowed above all of it. "Now! The boats are ready!"

Sebastian half-turned, seeing that it was true, then spun back in time to block a bayonet being thrust toward his stomach. He kicked the attacker away, swapped his empty pistol for a loaded one, and fired it into the crowd of foes.

"Pull back!" he yelled, hoping that the others there would hear him.

They did, men backing away from the fight as their foes continued to come after them. This close, the only blessing was that the ones on the cliffs couldn't target them, because their compatriots were too close. Sebastian went with the others, hacking at any man who came too close. A glance back said that the boats were fully in the water now, the oarsmen waiting despite the cannon fire. Sebastian didn't know how much longer they would wait, though.

"Run!" he yelled. "To the boats, hurry!"

The men with him took his instruction, running back in the direction of the shoreline. Sebastian ran with them, sheathing his sword now as he ran because it would only be in the way if he had to swim. He worked at the buckles of his breastplate for the same reason, discarding in on the sand as he followed his men to safety.

There was a boom, and something hit him like the kick of a horse in the side. Sebastian stumbled, and might have fallen if another man hadn't helped him to his feet. They ran together into the shallows, then deeper, and Sebastian could see his blood staining the water. He swam for the nearest of the boats, ignoring the agony that came with every stroke.

Hands reached down for him, and Sebastian let them haul him up. He found himself staring at Varkin, who looked down at him with obvious concern.

"Ignore it," Sebastian said. "Are the men aboard?"

"Yes, sir, but—"

"Then *row*!" he ordered.

They rowed, cannonballs striking the water around them in gouts of sea spume that reminded Sebastian of a whale surfacing. They rowed, and although the men were exhausted, they kept going, because the alternative was to sit there and wait for death.

Around him, men looked at him with something like awe as they rowed. Sebastian couldn't really understand it, because he'd only done what he assumed any man would.

"I told you that you'd save us," Varkin said. "Three cheers for his highness, lads!"

They cheered, and Sebastian wasn't sure that he'd ever been that embarrassed in his life. It felt good, too, though, to have the respect of men like this.

"It's going to be a long way home, sir," Varkin said.

Sebastian nodded. It would be—if they made it there at all.

CHAPTER EIGHTEEN

Kate hurried through the mercenary camp the way she hurried everywhere these days, because Lord Cranston seemed to want everything done at the double. Whether it was training with a blade, learning the disposition of the noble houses likely to employ a free company, or simply running errands around the camp, there was little time to do anything but run from place to place.

Her current task was to pick up equipment from the quartermaster after repairs. Hardly the kind of daring adventure Kate had hoped for, but she was starting to learn that war was often about boredom as much as violence.

She raced through the camp in her new uniform of a gray surcoat and dun breeches, using the errand as a way to practice moving through a crowd at speed, because Lord Cranston had told her to do exactly that. On other days, he'd had her sneak through the camp without being seen, or ride though on a borrowed horse, having to keep it in check despite the noise and the bustle of the place.

How long had she been there now? Long enough to fall into the rhythm of it, at least. Kate would wake early every morning, fetching Lord Cranston's breakfast and laying out clean clothes for him. Quite often, she would have to tidy away the wine skins from the night before as well. She would eat her own breakfast quickly, then move on to a seemingly endless string of errands, cut through with training with blade and bow, musket and pike.

Kate could pick up the thoughts of some of the men as she passed. Some of them were wary of her, having seen what she could do with a sword. A few thought there was something strange about the general having taken her on, and assumed that there must be more to it. More seemed to be thinking of her almost the way they might have thought about a lucky mascot, nodding as she passed.

Will was there too, polishing a blade with the expertise of someone who had been brought up around a forge. The bruises of his beating were faded now, leaving him as handsome as ever. He smiled as Kate approached.

"What does Lord Cranston have you doing today?" he asked.

"Running errands while running," Kate said.

"Probably practicing for a battlefield, where you'd be his best messenger," Will said.

That was what Kate had guessed. Lord Cranston had made it clear to her a dozen times now that she would never be a soldier fighting and dying in the line with the others, both because the men wouldn't accept it and because it would be a waste of her talents. Instead, he had her practicing in ways suited to a scout or a messenger, a bodyguard or even a leader.

"It's frustrating sometimes," Kate said. "I could stand with a pike."

"*Anyone* can stand with a pike," Will said. "That's the point of it. Not everyone can sneak through a camp or defeat half a dozen men single-handed."

That part was true, at least, and Kate had to admit that she wouldn't have been interested if her lot in the regiment had been to be just one more faceless figure acting in concert with the others. When they fought, there was something almost mechanical in the efficiency of thrusting pikes and volleys of projectiles. It was probably deadly, but it was also a long way from stories of daring warriors or dueling swordsmen Kate had heard.

"Can you stay?" Will asked, gesturing to a spot beside him.

Kate wished she could. There had been few enough moments to spend with Will since she'd found herself claimed as a member of his regiment. Lord Cranston kept her busy from morning to night, while Will had his own training to undergo, his knowledge of good metal earning him a place working with the company's two great brass cannon, loading and priming until it seemed as if he did nothing else.

"There's no time," Kate said. "He said to run there and back."

"Then you should," Will agreed. "I don't want to get you into trouble."

The *again* was unspoken, but with Kate's power, it was impossible to ignore.

"It's not your fault I ended up here like this," she said, reaching out to touch his arm. "And I like it here. It's everything I could have wanted."

She really did have to run then, heading off into the camp in the direction of the space where the quartermaster had his tent. Kate smelled it before she saw it, in the acrid stink of molten metal.

The quartermaster was waiting when Kate got there, pouring lead into molds to make shot.

"In some of the Merchant States, they build towers a hundred feet tall for this," he said, as Kate got there. "They drop lead down into buckets of cold water so that it ends up perfectly round. Must be something to see."

Kate imagined that it would be. She'd spent enough time around a forge to understand the sense of mystery that came from metal melting and flowing, hardening, and sharpening under the efforts of an expert. She was starting to suspect that the company's quartermaster was anything but that, but he seemed to know the right people to buy goods from, whether they were swords or potatoes, pistol flints or walking boots.

"Lord Cranston sent me to pick up his things," she said.

The quartermaster nodded, gesturing to a spot on a long bench. "I guessed that much. One reworked breastplate and two dueling pistols."

Kate went to the spot where they sat, the metal of the breastplate shining in the sun. Kate doubted that it would last, because it seemed that their camp turned to a thing of mud and drizzle-soaked clothes on a regular basis.

She picked up the breastplate, and she could see where it had been hammered back into smoothness after being dented in some battle or practice session. She could also see the more subtle signs in the way the sun reflected from it.

"There are cracks in this," Kate said.

She saw the quartermaster frown. "Where?"

Kate showed him. They were subtle, barely more than lines, but they were there. If a sword struck the steel there, it might shatter, and then Lord Cranston would find himself in trouble.

"Damn it," the quartermaster said. "I'll have to send it back out to be dealt with."

"Send it to the blacksmith Thomas," Kate suggested. "Will's father. He can fix it if anyone can."

She took the pistols at least, running back in the direction of Lord Cranston's tent. She had only a little time now. She paused as she saw a familiar face.

"Rosalind?"

Sure enough, the girl she'd saved from the House of the Unclaimed stood there, holding a basket of washing. She didn't wear the gray shift of the place now, but a rough-spun dress instead.

"What are you doing here?" Kate asked, shocked to see her in the company's enclosure.

"I had to go somewhere," Rosalind said, "and… I heard about you being here. I thought it might be safe. They needed washer women and cooks, servants and... well." She didn't finish that thought, but Kate could guess what she meant even before she looked into the other girl's thoughts. "I thought it might be safer here than in the city."

Kate wasn't sure if that was true or not, but she was at least glad that the other girl wasn't somewhere that the House of the Unclaimed might find her. Kate drew her close, into a hug.

"It's good to see you," she said. "Look, I don't have time to talk now, but if I find you later?"

She saw Rosalind nod. "I'd like that."

She sprinted the rest of the way back to Lord Cranston's tent. He was waiting, watching a now empty sand timer. Kate hadn't even known that there had been a time limit.

"What kept you?" he asked.

"There was a problem with your armor, sir," Kate said. "I've persuaded the quartermaster to get the cracks in it fixed properly."

"And you stopped to talk to at least two other people," Lord Cranston said, lifting a spyglass to emphasize the point.

"You never said that there was a time limit," Kate pointed out, a little annoyed that he would spend his time watching her like that.

"I told you to hurry," he pointed out. "In battle, the speed with which a commander gets information can determine who wins. Hesitating can cost lives, Kate."

She supposed she should have been used to Lord Cranston's methods by now. A day or two ago, he'd had her running errands around the camp while balancing an apple on her head, on the basis that a commander had to be able to maintain composure no matter what distracted them.

"You need to be careful around the boy," Lord Cranston said.

"You don't like Will?" Kate replied.

Not if he leaves you with child or with none of the men respecting you, Lord Cranston thought, although Kate gave no sign of having picked that up. He didn't need to know everything that she could do. *Not if he treats you like some of the lads treat the girls who come here.*

"He seems a fine enough lad," Lord Cranston said. "But... you need to be careful. I need you to concentrate on what you're learning."

"Why are you teaching me so much?" Kate asked. It didn't make sense, after she'd killed his men, that this nobleman should spend his time teaching her, but that was what he had done. There had been lessons on tactics and lines of command, on logistics and on fighting alongside others. It was a very different education from the one Siobhan had given her, but it was proving no less thorough, in its way.

"Maybe you remind me a little of myself when I was young," Lord Cranston said, although that didn't seem likely. It wasn't as though he'd been an orphan. He was the minor son of an even more minor noble. "Or maybe I can just see some of what is coming, and I want every weapon at my command I can get."

There was a note of worry there that caught Kate's attention.

"What *is* coming?" she asked.

Lord Cranston thought for a moment before he answered. "How much do you know about the wars on the continent? About our own wars?"

"Only a little," Kate admitted. In the orphanage, there had been no need for the girls to learn the complex details of the world's state, only the broad story of the Dowager and her family overcoming those who sought to overthrow her in the civil wars, with the aid of the Masked Goddess and the nobles, of course.

"A generation ago, we had the last throes in this land of a series of civil wars dating back two hundred years at their start," Lord Cranston said. "They started life as an argument by those families closest to the throne over which should succeed, and blossomed into something bigger, about whether a king or queen should rule at all, about whether there was a place in this land for those touched by the magic that once filled it, and whether people should be indentured simply for having been born in the wrong place and time."

He looked around, almost as if expecting some spy or informant to jump out and arrest him for sedition. That alone said something about how dangerous all of it still was. People spoke cautiously about these things, if they spoke at all.

"Here, the Dowager's family all but lost the argument," he said. "They were forced to accept the Assembly of Nobles, they were poised to declare freedom for those with small talents and an end to some of the injustices of the past. Then they got the support of the Masked Goddess's congregation, who could not stand to see these things destroyed. Overnight, a dozen of the most prominent supporting families died, and enough gold came in to give the Dowager's family at least some of its old status."

"It sounds as though it might almost be better if someone swept her away too," Kate said.

Lord Cranston raised a warning finger. "Don't ever say that where someone might hear. There are some things where even I can't keep you from a noose."

Kate nodded, but she still couldn't see the difference.

"Besides," Lord Cranston said. "The fact is that wars make things worse for the people who have to live through them. If an army were to rise here, even with the best of intentions, people would suffer."

"So why do you run a mercenary company again?" Kate asked.

Lord Cranston shrugged. "I like money, and in a war, it's probably safer to be a well-fed soldier than a starving farmer. Besides, if I fight across the Knifewater, I might be able to stop the wars coming here."

"And that's important?" Kate asked.

"Look at the continent. It is fighting over so many of the same issues that people aren't even certain which ones count anymore. The Disestablishers want no priests telling them what to do, and no crowns. The Merchant States want freedom to sell anything they wish, which sounds fine until you realize it includes people. The Old Empire, the True Empire, the Real Empire are all claiming a throne that disappeared a thousand years back, and want some version of what they call *tradition*."

"Again," Kate said, "they all sound as bad as each other."

With a dozen petty sides, who was she supposed to support? Who was she supposed to care about? War was supposed to be black and white, but this all seemed like a muddy mess.

"Some are very much worse," Lord Cranston assured her. "This New Army, for example, is something different. All the others, they stand for something, whether it's religion or country, merchant rights, or just honest profit. These… I'm still not sure what they stand for, or if they stand for anything. They just seem to *absorb*. They defeat armies, and they take them into their ranks. Room for everyone, and a noose for anyone who says no. They slaughter entire cities if they resist or refuse them. They are something that must be stopped, and yet I'm not sure if they *can* be. If they come here, too many people will die. They are utterly ruthless."

"You sound as though you admire them," Kate said.

Lord Cranston spread his hands. "If I admired them that much, I'd join them, but I do have *some* principles. And besides, they tend to kill officers to persuade the men to join. Their leader is a man they call Le Meistre de Corves in his own tongue."

The master of crows. Kate got the translation from the general's thoughts rather than from any knowledge.

"They say the crows follow wherever he goes," Lord Cranston said. "They say he sends a message by crow, and the world quakes."

"And what do you say?" Kate asked.

Lord Cranston shook his head. "I say men build reputations, and those can become weapons too. Talking of weapons…"

He took the dueling pistols, showing Kate how to check them and load them, moving over them with the kind of expertise that came from long practice. As he did it, he asked questions.

"What are the signs of the seven companies around Ashton at the moment?"

Kate knew that. "The star, the prancing horse, the bear, three chevrons, a blackened sun, the fish, and… oh, and your banner, sir."

"Thought you'd forget that one," Lord Cranston said. He passed her one of the dueling pistols. "Careful, it pulls to the left."

He took an apple and threw it up. Kate reacted on instinct, bringing the weapon to bear and firing, so that the apple exploded in a shower of fragments. The scent of smoke filled the world for a moment, and the roar of it was almost deafening. It was nowhere near as elegant as a bow or a blade.

There was something enticing about it though. There was something glorious in the way she could destroy the apple so simply and so powerfully. There was something wonderful in all the lessons Lord Cranston had to teach her, from the fine details of dueling to the proper way to wheel a company without exposing it to a charging foe.

This was what Kate wanted now. Siobhan had many things to teach her, but that seemed like the kind of fighting that minstrels sang about. This, there was something practical about it, something real. Kate would learn it, the way she learned everything else that came her way.

And if that meant being there when this New Army came calling, so be it.

CHAPTER NINETEEN

Sophia felt every bump in the road as the cart rumbled its way northward, out of the city. She looked back in fear, expecting to find a mob pursuing them at any moment. She wasn't sure what they could do if it happened. The cart couldn't outpace a running man, let alone a rider. As they rolled their way through the outskirts of the city, their safety felt like an ephemeral thing, a fine soap bubble likely to be destroyed at any moment.

I think we're safe, Emeline sent to her, and it was still strange, receiving sent thoughts from someone other than her sister.

"Who are you?" Sophia said. She realized how that must sound. "I'm sorry, you saved us, and I'm grateful. It's just…"

"You don't know why," Emeline said. "And you're worried that I'm only doing it because I have something worse planned."

Sophia nodded. It wasn't quite the whole of it, but it was a part of it. She'd seen more of the cruelty of the world than any kind of kindness.

"You said that you know my sister," Sophia said.

Emeline nodded. "I met her when I was trying to get out of the city on a barge. We ended up being thrown off it, and then I couldn't find her. When I heard your call for help, I knew I had to try to keep you safe."

"What call for help?" Cora asked, from the side.

Emeline frowned at that. "She doesn't know?"

Sophia knew she should have explained things to Cora, but she hadn't.

"Cora, there's something I have to tell you. I have a talent, a gift. I can see thoughts."

She saw Cora's eyes widen at that. "But that's… they used to call that witchcraft, in the orphanage. They say people who can do it feast on human blood."

"It isn't witchcraft," Sophia said. "At least, I don't think it is. I certainly don't drink blood, or anything like that. It's just… something I can do. Something Emeline can do too. I thought Kate and I were the only ones."

"Kate thought that too," Emeline said. "There are more like us than you think."

She said it as if it were nothing, when in fact it meant that the whole world was different from the way Sophia had thought. Cora looked even more shocked by the idea.

"You don't need to be afraid of us," Sophia said to her. "It doesn't make me any different. But if you want, I could stop the cart, and we could go in different directions." She paused only a moment. "I hope you don't, though. You saved my life."

She could have looked at Cora's thoughts to find the right things to say, but right then that would have felt like a betrayal. Instead, all Sophia could do was wait.

"I'll stay," Cora said at last. "You're right, you're still my friend. Maybe even a better friend to have now. And it isn't as though there's anything left for me in the city."

"Or me," Emeline said. "I've been trying to find a way out for a while now. There were places I was planning to go."

"What places?" Cora asked.

Emeline hesitated for a moment before she answered. "There's a place that is supposed to be safe for people like me. I want to find it. What about you? Where would you go if you could go anywhere?"

"I don't know," Cora said. "Somewhere I could be happy. Maybe an island somewhere."

There was only one place Sophia wanted to go right then, only one place that mattered.

"I'm going north," she said. "There's a house I have to find, in Monthys."

She saw Emeline frown at that. "Monthys is a long way north."

"It's practically in the mountains," Cora said. "What's so special about this house?"

Sophia didn't tell them all of it, because some of the details she'd had from Laurette van Klet seemed impossible. Still, she could give them the most important one.

"It was my parents'. I'll go there alone if I have to, but I *am* going."

Cora looked over at her. "I'll go with you," she said. "We're better off together."

"Emeline?" Sophia asked.

Emeline paused again, but then nodded. "I suppose if I don't know where I'm supposed to look for Stonehome, north is as good a way to look as any."

They went north, the cart continuing inexorably along roads that seemed to pass from cobbles to dirt and back again at random. At night, they slept beneath it, hobbling the horses in spaces with plenty of grass so that they could feed, taking fruit from the trees or wheat from the nearby fields for themselves. They supplemented it with supplies taken from the cart, or ones they traded for at the farmhouses they passed, swapping the beer that they'd hidden in for bread, cheese, and ham.

At the first of the inns they passed, Sophia managed to pick up the landlord's thoughts about her in time to simply turn around and walk out before he could grab for her. At the second, though, she managed to trade more of their stolen ale for sensible traveling clothes of dark wool.

They passed from the outskirts of the city into the Ridings, and then into the Shires beyond them. The Dowager's kingdom was not large compared to some of the great empires beyond the Knifewater, but to someone who had grown up within one small compound, and who had then seen little more than one large city, it seemed impossibly huge.

Huge, and varied. They rolled through fords and over bridges that looked as though they might have been there since the first inhabitants came to the island, and past standing stones that sat by the road, worn into odd shapes by centuries of the wind, with no clue as to what they'd originally been for.

They traveled for a day or more through a stretch that seemed to be nothing but open fields dotted with hamlets, then had to skirt around a town where so many merchant wagons rolled in that Sophia knew it had to be a market day. They passed through a marshy district where the spaces beyond the roads all gave way to water and reeds, and rolled through valleys between hills as they headed further north.

There were others on the roads, of course, although the three of them were careful about letting themselves be seen too often, because Sophia knew how vulnerable they would be to bandits or worse. When they heard riders coming, they would try to get off the roads if they could, but even so, they met tinkers and messengers, farmers traveling with their flocks and nobles traveling in closed carriages. On one occasion, they even traveled alongside a troupe of circus performers, heading up to Lonsford for its annual fair.

Gradually, the landscape started to change, becoming hilly and stone scattered, so that more of the farmers kept sheep or goats than cattle, and the cart became harder to free whenever it got caught in a rut. The streams here ran quickly, and Sophia began to see the watermills that were so popular in the north for grinding flour and more. Occasionally, they passed boats heading upstream, laden with goods from the south. They passed into one of the great forests there, thick with oak and elm and turning the light into a scattered, partial thing.

Ahead, Sophia heard mewling that sounded so much like a crying child that for a moment, she was convinced it was one. It was only as they got closer that she realized that it wasn't a child, but some kind of animal.

They rounded a bend in the road, and saw that it was indeed an animal, and not just any animal. A forest cat lay on its side, its left rear paw caught in a trap, the stripes of its long gray coat marred by blood. It wasn't full grown, because the biggest forest cats could take on wolves, but even so, it was the size of a large dog, sharp featured and beautiful.

And obviously in pain.

"We'll have to go around," Emeline said. "If we go near it, it will kill the horses."

"You can't just mean to leave it like that?" Cora said. "It's in pain."

"Not as much as we will be if we get too close," Emeline insisted.

Sophia drew the cart to a halt, stepping down.

"What are you doing?" Emeline asked. "There's no point in coming all this way if you're just going to get yourself eaten."

"Shh," Sophia said, focusing on the creature's thoughts. They were very different from anything human, and it seemed to take her an age to focus on them, picking them out against the background of a forest filled with other animal minds.

There were no words, of course. Human language had nothing to do with it, just feeling and intention and understanding. Right now, Sophia could pick out red-tinged pain and anger. She tried to send the idea of calm and safety across to it, and to her surprise, it seemed to work. She walked forward slowly, ready to jump back if it lashed out.

She laid a hand on its coat, feeling the warmth of it there as she ran her hands through its fur. She could feel how thin it was underneath, and how weak. How long had it been there like that? She jerked back as she heard a rumble that she took for a growl, then laughed as she realized the truth: the creature was purring the way any smaller cat might have.

Sophia reached for it again, pushing out soothing thoughts as she found the snare that had caught it. It was a horrific thing, set with wire rather than rope, and it seemed to take Sophia forever to cut through it with her short eating knife.

"There," she said, as the cat's leg came clear. "You're free now."

She expected it to run off, but instead, it lay there, looking at her in expectation.

"Cora," she said, not taking her eyes off it. "Do we have any meat back there?"

"I'll see what I can find," Cora said, and then she came forward, holding a couple of slices of salt beef, which she tossed down in front of the forest cat. It sniffed at it for a second, then gobbled the food up hungrily.

"You should go," Sophia said. "Go back into the forest."

It didn't go, though. Instead, it hobbled over in the direction of the cart.

"It's probably just after more food," Emeline said.

Cora tossed some more beef down, away from the cart, but the cat ignored it. When Sophia picked the food up and held it out, though, the great cat licked it from her palm as gently as a kitten might have. It was hard to remember that it was only a little more than that, in spite of its size.

"We can't take it with us," Emeline said.

The forest cat responded by clambering up awkwardly onto the cart, sniffing around for a while before turning and simply going to sleep.

"I'm not sure that we get a choice," Sophia said. She reached out, ruffling its ears gently. She wasn't frightened, because she felt sure that she would sense any intention to hurt them long before it happened and calm it. She flicked the reins and the cart started to move forward. Even then, the forest cat stayed curled up, half-asleep.

"Are you going to name it?" Cora said.

"Like some courtly noble with a yapping dog?" Emeline countered.

The forest cat was nothing like that, but even so, Sophia felt the temptation. "I think I'll call him Sienne. Would you like that?" Sophia asked the cat, ruffling its ears. It only purred in response.

"That's quite a talent you have," Emeline said. "They would probably love you in Stonehome."

Sophia frowned at that. "You mentioned it before, but what *is* this Stonehome?"

To her surprise, it was Cora who answered. "It's supposed to be a place for people who can do impossible things," she said. "I heard one of the nobles muttering about it once, saying that a servant who had run off had probably gone there. Everyone else shushed her. I don't think it's considered lucky to talk about it."

"It's not," Emeline agreed, "mostly because if you spend your time persecuting a group of people, finding out that they have built a city in the middle of your kingdom is probably terrifying."

"It's a whole city?" Sophia asked.

"I don't know," Emeline admitted. "I've never been there. I've never even met people who have. But I want to. Can you imagine somewhere where the priests won't call us witches, and people won't kick us in the street?"

Sophia wasn't sure that she could. She hadn't experienced the same cruelty as it seemed Emeline had, but only because she'd hidden her talent. She'd certainly heard the masked nuns preaching about the evils of those like her enough.

"It sounds like a good place," Sophia said.

"I hope it is," Emeline said. "You have to have some kind of hope."

"It sounds as though things were pretty hard for you," Sophia guessed.

Emeline nodded. "When my parents realized what I was, they threw me out of their home. I had to survive alone on the streets. I was usually fine right up to the moment when I guessed something that someone had only thought, not said. Then, they didn't want to know me, or they actually attacked me."

"I never had that," Cora said, "but I was given to the orphanage so young I barely remember my parents. When I was indentured to the palace, I was actually happy, because it seemed better than so many of the other things that could have happened. That was before I realized that to the nobles there, I would be nothing. Less than nothing."

"Maybe you could come to Stonehome too," Emeline suggested. "Maybe we could all go."

"I still want to find my parents' house," Sophia said.

She saw Emeline nod. "We'll do that first. But afterwards, promise me that we'll try to find it."

Sophia thought about that. A place designed for people like her seemed like an impossible dream. It seemed like something she could never hope to find, but if it was there, wasn't it worth trying?

"I promise."

CHAPTER TWENTY

Kate loved her training, whether it was the strange exercises of sneaking through the camp or the time spent learning tactics. But working with a sword was what she loved most of all. The problem was that after what had happened with the sword master, almost none of the soldiers there wanted to train with her, even with a practice blade.

Lord Cranston was different, and even though he didn't have the sheer strength and speed Kate had gotten from the fountain, he made up for it in all the tricks learned in a lifetime of fighting. Kate would find herself reeling back as he kicked dirt up in her face, or dodging away from thrown weapons, or caught by surprise as he pretended injury.

Kate learned only a few more of the subtleties of swordplay from the commander, but Lord Cranston taught her plenty about fighting in the midst of a battle. He made her train hemmed in on all sides, where she couldn't use speed and movement to avoid the attacks of her enemies. He made her learn the hack and thrust of violence without skill or beauty to it.

Even so, Kate thought she was doing well enough. She had more strength than her size should have given her, and more speed too, thanks to the fountain's effects. She had an instinct for the right moment to cut, and her time with Siobhan had taught her the moment to defend, if only because of all the ghostly blades that had pierced her flesh before.

"Where did you learn to do this?" Lord Cranston asked. "I can't imagine that they teach this kind of fighting in an orphanage."

"They taught me plenty about violence," Kate said. "But no, I learned this in the forest."

She didn't want to say much more than that until she was sure how Lord Cranston would react. The fact that he'd recruited her rather than killing her said that he was a practical man, but how would a soldier like him react to talk of magic?

"In the forest?" Lord Cranston asked. "Were you taught by the trees?"

He laughed at that, but Kate caught a flicker of his thoughts. He'd heard the old stories about the swordsman Argent, even if

122

he'd never really believed them. He was wondering about that now, and about what it might mean about Kate. If he knew that she could hear his thoughts like this, how would he react? Kate couldn't imagine that he would be happy. He might even believe that it placed his company in danger, having someone around who could pluck plans from his mind like that.

"Something like that," Kate agreed. "What's next?"

Lord Cranston appeared to think for a moment, then gestured to the flat practice field beyond the tents.

"What do you see?" he asked.

Kate frowned at that. She doubted that the answer was going to be a field. "I don't know, it's a field, it's flat—"

"Is it, though?" Lord Cranston asked her. "What about if I asked you to find cover in it?"

Kate looked around it and shook her head. "There's just grass."

"Look closer," Lord Cranston said. He lay down on his front and gestured for her to do the same. Kate did it, and stared out over the flat expanse of the grass without quite knowing what she was looking at.

Except that now she saw that it wasn't flat. Instead, small bumps and hollows dotted the field, with minor slopes and even a ridge partway across. Kate was surprised that she hadn't seen it all before.

"No landscape is truly flat," Lord Cranston said. "Even on the salt plains of Morgasa, there are variations in the ground, and a commander makes use of every one. Never ignore an advantage."

He started to show her where he would place men in defense and attack, how the small slope might provide marginal cover from arrow fire, and how a section of rabbit holes might be used to slow a charge just enough. Kate paid attention, even though she doubted that she would ever be in a position to command an army.

At least, she paid attention until she saw Siobhan standing among the nearby tents, simply staring at her. The woman of the forest was in a spot where she wouldn't attract attention, in spite of the plants that twined through her hair and the strange sense of power she exuded.

She was watching Kate and smiling with something like satisfaction, or possibly triumph. It was impossible to know when her thoughts were so closed off.

What are you doing here? Kate sent over to her, but there was no reply. Siobhan stepped back into the tents, and in a second, she was gone from sight.

Kate wanted to go after her, but how could she do it when Lord Cranston was in the middle of teaching her the details of how to set for a charge? More than that, how could Kate be certain that the witch would even be there when she caught up, rather than disappearing completely?

The big question was what she wanted. Was she just watching Kate's training, keeping an eye on her apprentice, or was there more to it than that? Kate doubted that she was doing it simply for the amusement value, although it was impossible to tell for sure with Siobhan. Kate started to try to think of excuses to look for her, perhaps claiming the need to run an errand, or offering to get a drink for Lord Cranston.

She was still trying to think of an excuse when a messenger ran onto the training field wearing insignia of the royal house. Kate stood hurriedly, although Lord Cranston took longer. Perhaps he cared less about what a messenger thought of him, or perhaps it simply took that long to straighten up, given a lifetime's worth of old injuries.

"What is it?" he asked the man, who stood there looking nervous.

Briefly, Kate found herself wondering if this might be about her. Had the priests gone to the palace to seek restitution? Perhaps the Dowager or the Assembly of Nobles was sending a message for Lord Cranston to hand her over. No, if that happened, she had no doubt that the priests would come themselves to enjoy the moment of her capture.

"Lord Cranston," the man said, holding out a letter, "the Dowager requests the services of your company."

Lord Cranston nodded to Kate. "Read it, would you?"

Kate was shocked that he would ask her to do that for him, and it seemed that the messenger was a little surprised too, because he clung on to the sealed letter until Kate pulled it sharply from his hands. The seal was a smaller version of the royal arms, with a portcullis in the shape of the island below a rose. Kate broke it open and read, picking through the spidery handwriting.

"It says…" She could hardly believe what she was reading, and so she read it again to be sure. "It says that enemy ships have been sighted off the shores of the kingdom, and as the royal forces are unavailable—"

"Practically nonexistent because the Assembly of Nobles won't allow them," Lord Cranston muttered while Kate continued to read.

"—your company is asked to take part in the defense of the realm. It prevails upon your honor, your commitment to the country, and your longstanding loyalty."

"Is that it?" Lord Cranston asked.

"There's a bit at the bottom saying that the messenger will answer any questions you have," Kate said. That made her turn her full attention to the man before them, and it was only as she caught more of his thoughts that she realized he wasn't just any messenger. The man was one of the more senior servants in the royal household. He'd obviously been sent there for a reason.

"Very well," Lord Cranston said. "Kate, what questions do you think we should be asking?"

Kate frowned at that, as did the messenger.

"I really don't think this is the time for some kind of lesson," the man said.

"There should always be time for lessons," Lord Cranston replied. "Kate?"

Kate tried to think. She didn't want to embarrass herself, or Lord Cranston. "Um... well, the obvious one is what enemy are we facing? How many? Where are they coming from?"

The messenger looked across to Lord Cranston, whose fingers stroked the end of his beard.

"Answer it, please. It will save a lot of time if you just assume that I know what I'm doing."

The messenger clearly wasn't happy about it, but he answered. "Reports state that it's an expeditionary force of the New Army, probably a couple of ships' worth at first, and likely to land somewhere between Ashton and Newspur Rocks."

"Which explains why they've come to us, Kate," Lord Cranston said. "We're here, after all, while the few royal forces are off doing... well, whatever it is soldiers do when they're being paid by the crown."

That brought Kate to another question. "I thought the crown couldn't raise soldiers directly without the Assembly of Nobles' permission?"

"Ah, an insightful one," Lord Cranston said, seeming pleased and steepling his fingers. "Well, young man, are we all to be hanged as traitors afterward, for seeking to build the power of the Dowager against her nobles?"

The messenger shook his head. "An emergency session of the Assembly's inner council was called, authorizing it. I have the papers here."

He held them out, and they did indeed seem to authorize raising troops.

"And now for the most important question," Lord Cranston said. He looked at Kate expectantly until, in the end, she cheated by plucking the answer from his thoughts.

"Are we getting paid?" she asked.

The messenger nodded. "I am authorized to offer your company up to ten thousand Royals, payable at the end of the conflict."

It was a considerable sum, but it wasn't the truth. Kate could see that much on the surface of the man's mind, and although she felt a little uncomfortable diving into the conversation even further, she couldn't help herself.

"Fifteen," she said, "with five payable immediately."

"Fifteen? I'm not—"

"Fifteen or we stay here and find better things to do than risk our lives," Kate said. "Lord Cranston was just teaching me all about grass, for example."

Actually, the man had been told he could go up to seventeen if required, but Kate thought that she should at least give him some chance to say he'd gotten a good deal.

"Fifteen," he agreed. "But your company is to mobilize within—"

"We will be at the most likely landing site within a few hours," Lord Cranston said, pushing on in the face of the other man's apparent disbelief. "A good commander shows up early to battle. That way, he gets to pick the ground he actually *wants*. Tell the Dowager that all is in hand, and that I expect payment promptly."

The messenger nodded, half-saluted, seemed to remember himself, and then left.

"You did well, Kate," Lord Cranston said. "Another lesson: loyal soldiers risk their lives for the love of their country and the sweethearts left behind, then get paid a pittance. A free company does it for a far more honest reason: for the money."

Kate wasn't sure that she agreed with the sentiment, but she *did* feel a little proud at having gotten Lord Cranston's company more coin than had been offered. She wasn't even sure if Lord Cranston really believed that it was just for the money, though. He'd said himself that the New Army needed to be stopped.

"Spread the message," Lord Cranston said. He raised his voice, so that others around the practice field might listen. "Sound trumpets, lads. I want you lined up in marching order in ten minutes! We're going to war!"

He might have set a fire in the middle of the camp, given the speed of everything that happened next. Men ran from their tents, shouting orders and hurrying to grab equipment. Soldiers who'd been practicing broke off from it with determined looks, knowing that the real thing was coming.

For her part, Kate found herself sent by Lord Cranston to prepare his armor and his weapons, his horse and his charts. She ran to prepare it all, and somewhere in it all she had to find enough time to ready her own blade and prepare for the possibility of what was coming.

There was no chaos to the way the company moved now. Instead, the various parts of it slid together like some perfectly judged mechanism, spilling soldiers onto the field in their tunics and occasional flashes of steel armor. Kate found herself looking for Will, and saw him helping to wheel one of the great brass cannons into place to chain them to a team of horses. She found herself wondering about Rosalind too. Would she be all right here alone? What would happen to her and those like her if these invaders broke through?

"Focus, Kate," Lord Cranston said. "I need you to pay attention. This is not practice now; this is war. You will need to be at your best, for all our sakes. The enemy is coming, and you will need to remember all you have learned."

Kate nodded, trying to focus on her orders. Lord Cranston was right: battle was coming, and she would need every scrap of skill she had in order to survive it.

CHAPTER TWENTY ONE

The journey across to the island had been long but essentially peaceful. The one back made Sebastian's arms burn with the effort of rowing, his stomach knot with the lack of fresh water, and his whole body tense with the terror that enemy ships might come hunting for their small boats at any moment. That was before he even began to consider the pain of the hastily bandaged wound in his side, or the cut on his cheek.

He didn't know why no enemies had come for them. Perhaps it was because they assumed that the small boats would be ripped apart by the waves in the course of the crossing. Perhaps it was because their commanders had better things to do than chase a retreating force. That was a worrying thought in itself, because it made Sebastian wonder what those better things might be.

The only thing he could think of was beating the small boats back to the kingdom.

The landing craft they rowed were sturdy things for their size, but they certainly weren't designed for the journey across the Knifewater. Waves washed into their tiny flotilla, so that they had to bail with helmets and the remains of armor that was no more than dead weight otherwise. Partway across, a man washed overboard, and the weight of the breastplate he still wore dragged him down before it was even possible to think about turning to help him. One of the boats capsized as something struck it from underneath, and at least one man was pulled under the water in a spreading cloud of blood before they managed to right it. Sebastian never even saw what the creature was that had done it.

It was a few dozen miles of water, but right then it felt like an eternity. Sebastian and the others rowed, but the truth was that they were a tiny thing against the sheer scale of the sea around them, barely able to control where they went in the face of the wind and the currents.

When the familiar pale cliffs of his mother's kingdom came into view, Sebastian could only count it as a minor miracle. Several of the other men proclaimed it exactly that, shouting their thanks to the Masked Goddess and declaring that they would donate to her temples as soon as they were safe enough to reach them.

Sebastian knew it wasn't done yet. It was one thing to spot a coastline, but quite another to find a safe spot to land on it. They still had to row the distance into shore without being dashed on rocks or pulled back out into the strait. He thought he saw buildings dotting one stretch of the shore and pointed.

"There. Aim for them."

It took another hour. Another hour of blistered hands and backbreaking rowing, of the heat of the sun bearing down and the salt water rasping at his skin. With the waves around them rising to their familiar sharp peaks, Sebastian was certain that their boats must capsize in the face of it.

Somehow, they made it into shore, on a shale landing slope that was dotted with fishing boats and led up to rows of houses. Sebastian all but fell out of the boat, held up by the hands of men who didn't seem much steadier.

"You got us back," Sergeant Varkin said, sounding astonished. "I was sure we were going to die, but you brought us home." He clasped Sebastian's hand. "I'll not forget that, your highness. None of us will."

Sure enough, the other men crowded round, at least half of them wanting to shake his hand. Sebastian wasn't sure that he deserved it. Without his presence, there would have been no ill-conceived scheme to attack the island. As for their escape, it had been as much about the strength of the men as anything he'd done.

He looked up and suspected that his work might not be done. Soldiers ringed the small landing space, or at least the kind of irregulars who passed for it when there was nothing better. Half of them looked like fishermen pressed into hurried service, with harpoons and bill hooks that still looked wickedly sharp for all that.

"Who goes?" a man called down.

"Prince…" Sebastian's voice was cracked with the effort and the lack of water, but he forced authority into it with an effort. "Prince Sebastian and the royal army. Look at the uniforms if you don't believe me!"

He was grateful in that moment that they weren't one of the free companies; that they actually wore the blue, gray, and gold of the royal house. Combined with their voices, it was enough to make the men above pause, then stand back as Sebastian came forward.

"Goddess," one of them said. He was a round man who looked more like a merchant than a soldier. "It *is* him! I saw him at a trade dinner once. Your highness, forgive us, we didn't know it was you."

Now that they knew who he was, fear gave way to a kind of awe. A couple of men even attempted rough salutes.

Sebastian waved that away. "You did what I would expect you to do, and what you might need to do again, soon enough."

"Is there anything we can do for you and your men?" the merchant soldier asked. "Water, food?"

Sebastian nodded. "My men will appreciate that," he said. "What I need, though, is the fastest horse you can find me. My mother needs to hear what happened here."

***

By the time Sebastian reached Ashton, riding at full tilt, he felt as though he might tumble from his horse in exhaustion. Did he really need to push himself so hard, when the village had sent messages ahead of him with fresh horsemen and carrier birds?

Probably not, but Sebastian wasn't going to shirk his duty. If the New Army's fleet didn't have the time to hunt down his fleeing boats, what were they doing instead? One possibility was obvious: they were moving ahead with an attack. He had to bring the warning.

So he thundered through the streets of the city, barely possessing the strength to keep clinging to his horse as he made his way to the walled precinct of the palace. There was a delegation of courtiers and servants waiting for him, and Sebastian guessed that the messages must have gotten through. He should have expected it.

What he didn't expect was the applause.

They clapped and cheered as he rode between them, offering bows and curtseys as he stumbled from his horse with what felt like all the grace of a sack falling from a cart. They chattered around him, offering congratulations, wine, even a garland of flowers better suited to one of the conquering heroes of some ancient land.

Sebastian realized then that this reception wasn't some spontaneous outpouring of affection. It was one that had probably been planned almost before he set off for the Strait Islands, there to celebrate his glorious victory over a bunch of farmers. That there was now a real victory to celebrate only made the whole thing seem more hollow.

"Your highness!" a noble girl exclaimed in what was practically a shriek of delight. "You've been wounded!"

She probably meant that it looked very dashing, but Sebastian couldn't help wondering if she would have been even happier had the musket ball struck a little higher, giving her an excuse to break out her finest black dresses for the mourning to follow.

"Excuse me, please," Sebastian said, pushing through them, yet they seemed so reluctant to part that for a moment Sebastian had memories of being hemmed in by enemy troops. The difference was that he wasn't allowed to cut *these* ones down.

"Out of the way, all of you," a woman's voice called, and Sebastian was astonished to see Milady d'Angelica pushing her way through the crowd toward him. She looked surprisingly restrained in the way she was dressed today, in a simple and elegant cream dress rather than her usual elaborate confections. She pushed her way through to him, reaching out for his arm without being asked. "Can't you see that he's practically falling down?"

She supported him as they pushed through the crowd, and that was a shock in itself. Sebastian had never conceived of Angelica being kind or supportive in any way, let alone all but shoving aside minor nobles to get him to safety.

"What have you done to yourself?" she asked, and Sebastian could hear what sounded like genuine concern there. "I know you were going off to prove yourself, but *this*?"

Sebastian was only too aware of how he must look, in his disheveled uniform crusted with blood. He guessed that he probably didn't smell any better, after so long spent rowing across the Knifewater. He certainly couldn't smell half as good as Angelica did, with the kind of subtle perfume that spoke of flowers and honey, expense and just a hint of more than that.

"I'm sorry, your highness," she said. "I know I'm forgetting propriety with all this. It's just something of a shock to see you like this. I hope you don't mind me helping?"

"No, I'm grateful for it," Sebastian said, as they passed into the palace proper. Still, there were people on every side, applauding him as if he'd presided over a glorious victory rather than a hasty retreat. He sighed. "They're all acting as if I singlehandedly won all the wars on the continent at once."

He saw Angelica smile at that, and he had to admit that she had a beautiful smile.

"From what the messengers were saying, you saved your men when it looked as though you were all going to die. I think that probably counts for something. Come on, let's get you to your rooms to clean up."

Sebastian shook his head. "I have to go to my mother. I have to explain everything that happened."

"*After* we make sure that you aren't bleeding to death," Angelica said, and then had another moment where she seemed to realize what she was saying. "I'm sorry, but it's just worry. Your mother will have heard the reports from the messengers by now, and I'm sure she'd want to make sure you're whole. Besides," she wrinkled her nose slightly, "even her son can't go in front of the Dowager in *that* state."

Sebastian knew that Angelica had a point, so he kept hold of her arm as he made his way to his rooms, leaning on her probably more than he should have. At the door, he started to pull back, but she kept a grip on him.

"Oh no," she said. "Not until I'm sure that you're safe."

Sebastian frowned at that. "That wouldn't be—"

"Proper?" Angelica asked. "Don't worry, Sebastian, I'm not about to seduce you when you can barely stand. And it isn't as though my reputation needs to be protected."

She laughed at it as if it were nothing, but then her expression turned more serious.

"Besides," she said, "there are things I need to talk to you about."

They went inside, and Sebastian ducked behind a dressing screen to clean his wound as best he could. He removed his shirt and set to work with a bowl of water, cleaning away the blood from the edges of the wound and gently peeling back the cloth he'd used to cover it.

"Here, let me help with that," Angelica said.

"You can't…" Sebastian said, shocked that she would be there like that.

"Oh, don't be silly," she said. She took the washcloth from him and dabbed at the edges of the wound, making Sebastian hiss in pain. "*Sebastian*. This isn't some neat little dueling scar. A little further over and you might have been killed!"

"I shall have to ask the enemy to be more careful next time," he said. He took a fresh shirt out from a drawer, pulling it on so that at least he might be covered and there might be some propriety there.

"Or they'll have me to answer to," Angelica said with a smile.

This was a side of her that Sebastian hadn't seen. He was so used to her being arch and formal, fighting her way up through the realms of the court in a battle that was still vicious for all that it was fought with words rather than knives.

That reminded him…

"You said that there were things you needed to tell me," Sebastian said. He saw Angelica look away. "What is it?"

"It's about Sophia," she said. She sounded worried. "I don't… maybe I shouldn't say anything, but I thought you would want to hear it from me, rather than just as a rumor."

That caught Sebastian's interest. He guessed that it would be something to do with the House of the Unclaimed. Perhaps people at the palace had finally worked out where she'd come from, or they'd heard about the things Kate had done there.

"What happened?" Sebastian demanded.

He saw Angelica take a breath. "She... came back here. She was dressed very strangely, almost... if it had been anyone else, I'd have said that she was dressed like a courtesan. She was angry too. She had a knife, and she was talking nonsense about how much she hated you, and how she needed to find you."

Sebastian shook his head. "That doesn't sound like her."

"I know it's hard to believe," Angelica said. "She seemed so gentle when she was here, but it seemed... it seemed as though something had happened to her, and she blamed you for it. There's more though. She couldn't find you, but she found Prince Rupert."

Sebastian's jaw clenched at the thought of all the ways that could have gone. He knew his brother.

"What happened?"

"They say she attacked him," Angelica said. "She couldn't find you, so she hurt him instead. It might not be true, but... well, Rupert *was* hurt, and the guards were alerted. They were chasing after her."

Sebastian kept shaking his head. None of this sounded like Sophia. Yet... how well did he really know her? He hadn't even known who she was until Laurette van Klet painted her. Was it possible that she really *did* hate him?

Just the possibility of it felt as though it broke something in him. It felt as though the world was slipping away, the ground below dropping into a pit of loneliness and pain from which there could be no escape.

Sebastian felt Angelica's hand settle on his shoulder.

"I know it's hard," she said. "I know you cared about her, but whatever happened between you, maybe it's for the best. What *did* happen?"

Sebastian shook his head. He couldn't tell anyone that. "It doesn't matter."

"No," Angelica agreed, "it doesn't. You still have your future in front of you, Sebastian. She's just some angry girl who can only react with hatred. Now, we've probably kept your mother waiting long enough. You should go to her."

"I should," Sebastian agreed. "She needs to hear this from me."

"And who knows?" Angelica said. "Maybe she'll have some news for you too."

CHAPTER TWENTY TWO

Sophia ached as she worked to push the cart out of yet another rut with the others. She'd thought that the roads around Ashton were uncomfortable, but the further north they went, the worse the roads seemed to get. The Dowager clearly didn't care to spend money on roads she would never tread.

Right now, Sophia wished that she had.

"Almost... there," she said, as the others pushed along with her. Even Sienne the forest cat had jumped down, lightening the load more than a little. The cart rumbled forward, pulling out of the deep hole in the road that gripped it fast enough that Emeline had to run to grab the reins before they lost it.

"How much further?" Cora asked.

Sophia didn't have an answer for that. Whenever they passed travelers, they asked the direction of Monthys, so they knew that they were heading in the right direction, but there was no sense of how far it was, only the endless road.

It had been the same way for days now, with the going only getting tougher as they traveled. Weather that had been fine as they had set out had now turned to nearly constant rain and wind, so that even finding dry wood for a fire was hard some nights, and there were moments when Sophia felt as though she'd been dunked in a river. When that happened, Sophia pulled herself closer to Sienne, enjoying the soft warmth of the cat's presence close to her.

There were other, more difficult aspects to having the creature traveling with them. They had salt beef in one of the barrels, but only so much of it, and Sienne still wasn't strong enough to hunt for himself, even if he did hop down from the cart at the sight of rabbits by the road. It meant that they had to hunt small animals as they went, and Cora turned out to be surprisingly good with a short hunting bow that Emeline pulled from the cart.

Sophia was surprised by how well she got along with the two girls. In the orphanage, it had always just been her and Kate, and anyone else was suspect because of the violence of the place. In the palace, Cora had been her friend, but with everyone else, she'd had to keep her real self hidden. Here, it felt as though she finally had the space to enjoy the simple moments of friendship, whether it was laughing at Emeline's attempts at singing made up songs as they went along, or enjoying Cora's wonder at finally being somewhere outside Ashton.

Even so, she found herself wishing that they could find her parents' old home. She wanted to find out how much truth there was in the words of Laurette van Klet, and just what had happened to her family. It seemed as though every day brought fresh obstacles.

Right now, the obstacle was a river.

They had crossed rivers before, but this was deep and fast flowing, impossible to risk fording. Sienne walked up to the edge of it then turned away from it, hopping back onto the cart in obvious disgust at that much water.

"What now?" Cora asked.

"There will be a way to cross," Emeline said. "There always is."

Sophia had to take her word for it, and to be fair, Emeline was the one who had spent the most time on the great river running through the city. They set off parallel to the bank, choosing to go downstream on the basis that the route upstream sloped too sharply, and Sophia hoped that it wouldn't be too long before they found a way across.

It took less than an hour before they came to the spot where a ferry sat by the bank, a long rope strung across the river to hold it in place and allow those using it to pull their way to the far bank. It didn't look like the safest way to cross a river, but Sophia couldn't see any other options, and at least the ferry raft looked large enough to hold their cart.

They dismounted to lead the horses onto it with the cart behind them. The rope was a thick, hempen thing that felt to Sophia as if it would tear at her hands with every pull on it, but she and the others gripped the thick rope and strained against it to haul the ferry forward.

On land, they could never have moved the cart like that. Whenever they'd been stuck in a rut, it had taken all of them and the horses too. On water, it wasn't easy, but it was at least possible. They pulled themselves forward for minute after minute, crossing the rapid flow of the river.

There are people over there, Emeline sent to her. *I can feel their thoughts.*

Sophia stretched out her own talent, and sure enough, she could pick out the thoughts of a trio of men, all waiting with a kind of

135

vicious anticipation. Even as she spotted them, they stepped out onto the far bank. She heard Cora gasp, and realized that she should probably have warned her about what was coming.

The men wore rough-spun clothes, and had the bulky set to them of farmers, although the knives they held and the masks they wore across their lower faces said that they were robbers. One, in particular, had the roughness to him of a man who had seen too many fights, while the other two seemed younger. Brothers perhaps, drawn into this because the eldest had decided it. Sophia snorted at that thought. Kate would never do what Sophia said simply because she was the eldest.

"Stop where you are!" the oldest one yelled. "There's a toll on this river, and you'll pay it, or we'll cut the rope and leave you to it."

Sophia stopped, along with the others. She glanced around at the river. It was flowing fast now, and she suspected that if the rope were cut, they wouldn't just drift safely to shore.

"We'll drown if that happens, won't we?" she asked Emeline.

Emeline nodded. "Probably."

"We can just head back," Cora suggested, but Sophia knew that wouldn't work. These men could cut them loose whichever way they headed.

Instead, she turned her attention to the men.

"What's the toll?" she demanded.

She could feel the satisfaction roiling off their robbers. Their leader cocked his head to the side, considering it. Sophia could see some of the things he was considering, but if he dragged them to shore to try to do any of them to her and the others, she'd kill him. She'd felt a mind like that before with Rupert, and she wouldn't let another close.

"Any coin you have!" he said at last, obviously guessing the dangers.

They didn't have much. They'd traded for some using the beer that had been on the cart, and Emeline had a little anyway, but even so, it amounted to a couple of dozen Royals, no more than that. When they tossed them across the open water, though, the men there looked at them as if they'd found a fortune. Perhaps here in the countryside, it was.

They laughed and put the coin away, and Sophia thought that they might simply leave then. It was what the two younger ones wanted, thinking of an inn with a broken wheel for a sign. The older had other ideas, though. If he couldn't get them to shore to have his fun, then...

"No!" Sophia yelled, as he reached for the rope. "Cora, Emeline, hold on!"

He cut the rope, and Sophia felt the raft lurch, freed from the control the line gave it. She heard the horses whinny in fear, and she started to search the cart, looking for anything that it might be possible to use as an oar. The best that Sophia could think of was one of the last barrels, and she tore at it, trying to break it apart.

"We need oars," she told the others, and they joined her, pulling at it. Already, the raft was spinning away downriver, caught by the current. Finally, the barrel broke, and Sophia gripped one of its slats, using it as a paddle as she pulled at the water.

"Not against the current," Emeline said, joining her. "Aim for the bank."

Cora joined in, each with a makeshift paddle trying their best to steer the course of the raft. The water splashed over the side, and Sophia felt sure that it must tip, but it didn't. Slowly, by inches, they pulled it in toward the shore. It helped that they had only been a short distance away when the rope was cut, a few dozen strokes of the oars.

It made what the bandit farmer had done seem almost forgivable. Almost.

Finally, they made landfall in a scrape of wood against rock. They drove the cart forward, not caring that the horses were terrified by it. They thundered onto dry ground, and Sophia called Sienne to her with a flicker of her thoughts, daring to breathe again as she held her.

"We're safe," Cora said, obviously barely able to believe it. "It's over."

Sophia shook her head. "It isn't over."

If they'd just taken the money, she might have left this alone, but cutting the rope... that could have killed them. She couldn't let that go.

***

It took two hours to find the inn with the broken wheel sign. It was just a normal small inn, in the middle of a village barely big enough to warrant it. Sophia pulled the cart to a halt in front of it, tying the horses in place. She stood outside for a while, listening in the way that only she could listen, and planning.

"Emeline, Cora, go around the back," she said when she was sure that she understood what was going to happen next. "The men have rooms here. I want you to steal back what they took while I distract them."

"And what will you be doing?" Emeline asked her.

Sophia didn't have a good answer for that. "I'll be going in the front."

It sounded like the kind of thing her sister might have done, but Sophia wasn't thinking the same way. She wasn't going to charge in and fight, but she wasn't going to leave this either. She was going to find another way. A clever way. She'd done it at the palace, after all.

When she walked in, all the eyes there turned to her. She'd half-expected, half-hoped that. This was a small village in the middle of nowhere, after all. Farmers in from the fields were drinking, but only a few so far. Sophia was just interested in the trio of figures toward the back, drinking more and gambling among themselves with a portion of the stolen money.

They stared at her now, and without their masks they looked younger. There was still something cruel about the eldest of them though. The younger two looked at Sophia as if they'd just been caught shirking by their mother. The older one looked as though he'd just found an unexpected rabbit in a trap.

"What's wrong?" Sophia asked. "Didn't expect to find me here after you tried to kill me?"

"You've no proof of that," the older one said. "No point even trying to go to a magister."

Sophia laughed at the thought of her getting anything like justice from a court that would probably give her back to slavers the moment it saw her.

"I don't do things that way," she said. She nodded to the game. "I thought I'd try getting back what I'm owed a better way. You like to gamble?"

"Aye, I like to gamble," the oldest said. "But what have you got to gamble with?"

Sophia swallowed. "Myself. You were thinking about it at the river, weren't you? You wanted me. One night, against what you have here."

She could see him considering it. He wanted it. The question was how much.

"What game?" he asked.

"A guessing game. You put dice under your cup, and I'll guess odd or even. If I guess right, I win the money. If I guess wrong…"

She let that hang, giving him time to think about it.

"All right," he said. He pushed a pile of money into the center of the table, then started to arrange dice under an upturned cup. Sophia watched him calmly, thinking about the next part of it. "Ready."

Sophia tried to make it look like a guess. She made it look as though she was agonizing over it, rather than just picking it from his mind. In the end though, she just said it.

"Evens."

She watched him redden as she lifted the cup away for the others in the inn to see. She plucked up the coin quickly, putting it away. She turned to leave…

…and felt his hand fasten on her arm.

"Double or quits," he said. "You against twice the coin."

The others there murmured. His brothers looked at him as if knowing what a bad idea it was. One started to speak, but the eldest cut him off.

"Shut up," he said. "You wouldn't even have money without me."

He put a pouch down on the table.

"Very well," Sophia said. She knew she shouldn't do this, but by this point, it wasn't about the money.

Again, he arranged the dice. Again, Sophia watched his thoughts carefully.

"Even again," she said. "But you're planning to tilt the dice as you lift the cup. Don't try to cheat me."

She reached out, snatching the cup away. Just as fast, she lifted the money pouch. She stood then.

"You're done here when I say you're done here," he said. "You think you get to come in here and just take back what I stole? You think you get to walk out of this? The game doesn't matter. I'm going to take you, and—"

"There's someone I'd like you to meet," Sophia said, interrupting him calmly. "This is Sienne."

She sent a flicker of thought, and the forest cat stalked into the inn. Sophia heard the gasps around her. The man's brothers slunk back against the wall in fear. Most of the inn's inhabitants gave ground at the sight of the predator.

"I'd say that you had one chance to let go of me," Sophia said. "But you used up your chances back at the river, when you tried to kill me and my friends. Sienne, attack."

The forest cat leapt forward, snarling. The thug fell back, his screams rising in intensity as claws and teeth sliced into him.

"That's enough, Sienne," Sophia said, calling her back. The forest cat slunk back to her side, licking blood from his paws. The would-be thief lay on the ground, moaning in pain. Sophia felt no pity for him. Instead, she moved to kneel by him, drawing a knife.

"All my life," she said, "I've had people thinking that they can do what they want with me. They think that they can take what they want without consequences. They think that they can try to kill me. You made a mistake though. You left me alive."

She left him, but not out of any sense of mercy. She simply didn't want people hunting for her and the others. She left him ravaged by claw marks, standing with the knife still in her hands. This was the reason that she'd sent the others around the back. She hadn't wanted them to see this. She hadn't wanted them to stop her. She might not live for vengeance the way Kate did, but she was sick of being so weak that people thought they could take advantage of her.

She looked around at the faces of the farmers there, marred by terror and anger in equal parts.

"This man is a thief, a killer, and a would-be rapist," she said, as they tried to make up their minds whether to stop her. "Not one of you tried to stop him. If you try to stop me from leaving, you'll get the same justice he did."

She stalked out, and managed to keep from shaking until she made it to the cart.

CHAPTER TWENTY THREE

Kate fidgeted as she waited behind the rocks, staring out over the ocean. She tried to make herself into a thing of unmovable rock, still as the chalk cliffs nearby. It didn't work though. She'd been waiting there too long for that.

"Nine-tenths of warfare is waiting," Lord Cranston said, in the rocks not far from her. He wasn't crouched and stiffening like Kate and the others there, but was instead sitting comfortably on a camp stool he'd arranged for the purpose. He was even reading a book of what appeared to be poetry, occasionally reading sections aloud in Ancient Helene as if Kate would understand.

"It feels as though we're working on the other tenth as well," Kate complained. Birds wheeled overhead, the waves crashed on the shore, and still there was no sign of their enemy. Down in the rocks, their men had taken up positions that wouldn't give away their presence. Even the cannon had been covered with foliage to disguise them.

"Now wouldn't that be a thought?" Lord Cranston said. "Warfare without the awkward business of being shot at." She heard him sigh. "Sadly, I don't think it will be happening today. Look."

Kate looked out over the water, following the line of Lord Cranston's pointing finger. As she watched, she saw ships go from dots to more obvious shapes, landing boats swarming from them like ants from a nest. They moved in closer with rapid, synchronized strokes, and Kate braced herself for the moment when they would land.

So did the others. She could see men readying weapons, loading muskets and drawing swords for closer work, the tension building. Still, the whole beach was quieter than Kate could have believed, so that she could even hear the cawing of the birds above the rest of it.

One landed close to her, and Kate found herself staring into the eyes of a large black crow.

"Like the Master of Crows you were telling me about," she said.

"What's that?" Lord Cranston asked. Kate saw him look across at the crow, and she could feel his concern rising. "Crows aren't seabirds. There's something wrong."

Soldiers appeared, moving down the beach at speed, and Kate knew then that they'd been spotted. The landing parties were a distraction.

They turned to face the new foe, but their lines were set to take on an enemy force coming from the sea, not one coming at them from the land. They were still reorganizing when the enemy lifted muskets and fired, filling the air with lead and acrid smoke. Men fell, screaming. Something whizzed past Kate's ear, taking a chip from the nearby rocks.

"Return fire!" Lord Cranston yelled above the noise of it all, and whatever good humor he'd had before had disappeared now. Kate heard the crack of flintlocks, and the thud of arrows. She jumped up, firing a pistol, and saw a man fall in response. Above her somewhere, a cannon boomed, and she found herself thinking of Will, hoping that he would be all right.

Then the landing boats hit the shore, and there was no time to think of anything else but survival.

"Go to the men there," Lord Cranston said, pointing. "Tell them to pull back to my position. Do it now!"

Kate nodded and set off, sprinting and dodging as projectiles flew around her. A man in an ochre tunic came at her and she ducked under the swing of a sword, coming up with her own already drawn to plunge it into his back. She sensed a flicker of hostility from her left and barely brought her weapon around in time to bat away another sword, kicking an attacker away.

On another occasion, Kate might have followed that up, pressing forward for the kill, but she had an order to fulfill, and just the tone of Lord Cranston's voice had been enough to impress on her the importance of it. Kate could see it for herself. The men who had wheeled to meet the attackers on the beach had set themselves against that new threat, only to leave themselves vulnerable to the ones coming in the boats.

They needed to pull back, but already, the ones from the boats were starting to form a firing line, ready to bring down all the soldiers who were caught out in the open. That included Kate, who was too far out now to be able to find cover.

She did the only thing she could think of, taking emotion and throwing it at the men the way she had with some of Siobhan's constructs back in the forest. She took all the pain and confusion she could find, from the horror of her first kill to her earliest memories of fire and pain. She flung it like a net, catching as many men as possible in it, and she saw them stagger, stunned by it if only for a few seconds.

"Pull back!" she yelled to the men on her side, and to her surprise, they listened. Perhaps they'd just gotten used to her running errands for Lord Cranston, and now they didn't question it when she spoke for him. Maybe he'd known what he was doing, having her run all over camp on his behalf.

Whatever the reason, they started to pull back, while in front of them, the soldiers in the ochre tunics fumbled with their weapons, not quite able to bring them to bear as they struggled with everything Kate had thrown at them.

They sprinted back to the rocks, and Kate went with them, catching a straggling enemy with her blade without even slowing down. There was no time to fight then, only enough to hit and run, leaving a wound that would probably take the man out of the fight for a while at least as she ran for the cover of the rocks.

Kate made it to them as the effects of her mental attack started to wear off, shots sounding now as Lord Cranston's men started to fling themselves into cover. Some weren't quick enough, falling as lead balls hit them. Kate saw a man go down just in front of her, and she rushed from the rocks, dragging him back while stone chips flew around her.

From their cover, Lord Cranston's men fired back in staggered volleys, designed to allow the men who weren't firing enough time to reload. The archers filled in the gaps with arrows, and the cannon above fired again, sending up sprays of wooden splinters as they shattered the landing boats below.

It seemed like an impossible storm of violence, and Lord Cranston stood in the middle of it as calmly as if he were taking a stroll, shouting orders and trying to marshal the response. Despite it all, Kate could see that it wouldn't be enough. There was no way that it could be. She'd saved the men on the beach and allowed them enough time to regroup, but even dug in, there was no way for them to stand against so many opponents.

Then Kate felt power rising up inside her that she didn't understand. It felt as though she could feel everything around her, from the heartbeats of the men to the curl of the waves nearby. She felt connected to it all completely, and somehow, she knew that it was hers.

Siobhan had told her once that weather magic was not for her, but in that moment, Kate instinctively understood it. That scared her a little, because she suspected that the forest woman would not be happy that she understood that kind of power untrained, but right then she didn't care. She reached out with a tendril of power, and then the mist began to rise.

It began slowly, in curls of vapor that mingled in with the smoke of the firing weapons, but Kate found it growing, mingling with dark clouds and drizzling rain that wet the powder and the sand alike.

Slowly, it grew, until Kate could only see a few paces in front of her, and the enemies disappeared in it. At least, they did for everyone else. In this thick fog, it was like being in the thick forest, unable to see far ahead, but able to hear, and touch, and pick out the distinctive signatures of minds.

Without a word, she slipped into the mist, her sword ready for what was to come.

Kate picked a spot where the clustering of minds was thinnest, running forward in silence. A figure came out of the mist, looked shocked at her sudden appearance, and tried to raise a sword. Kate struck him through the throat and kept running, already away in the mist by the time shouts sounded behind her.

She struck at another man in the mist, and this time he was quick enough to get a blade up to parry. He sliced back at her, and Kate swayed away from the stroke, barely avoiding it. She thrust, and then rolled her wrist to take her saber around her opponent's parry, hacking into his arm.

Again, she ran on.

Kate sprinted from spot to spot, feeling for the spaces where the enemies were the most spread out, picking off stragglers wherever she could and then disappearing as men rushed forward, trying to catch up with the one who struck at them from nowhere. She hit a group of them next, coming in from behind to cut down one man, then thrusting through the chest of another as he turned to face her before running back into the mist.

It seemed as though she was the predator then, and they the prey, but Kate knew just how dangerous a game this was. She could feel the men trying to coordinate with one another to find her, even as she could feel their fear rising. She needed to be silent and deadly with every attack, killing and then moving away again before they could come at her in numbers. They just needed to tangle her up in violence for a few seconds, while more of them could turn to fight against her.

Kate kept running, kept killing, kept hoping that what she was doing would be enough.

Around her, shots started to sound as men who hadn't dared to fire in the mist before risked it in the face of the silent killer stalking them. Booms erupted as men fired at shadows or flickers of smoke, and musket balls hit the sand around Kate, sending up showers of it.

Kate could feel men watching for her now. There were groups of them huddling together, their weapons ready, and Kate could pick up the poised readiness in their thoughts, prepared to fire arrows and musket balls at the least provocation. That gave Kate an idea, and she smiled grimly as she crept between the two largest groups, waiting for her moment.

"Here!" she yelled at the top of her voice, then threw herself flat.

The world erupted around her, with men firing blindly from both sides. Some screamed as their own side shot at them. Some of them, thinking that it was the enemy, continued their attack. Projectiles flew above Kate, close enough that she was sure one must strike her in a second or two, yet there was only the sound of men dying all around her.

An officer's voice called for the men to cease their fire, but it was in vain at first. He yelled it louder, but Kate guessed that it was the need to reload more than any real obedience that brought the cacophony to a halt.

Kate rose from her belly and ran, knowing that she would only have moments before men closed in on the spot where she'd been standing with steel. She felt for the minds ahead of her, and already there were men moving to cut her off. She leapt at one in the mist, but it was starting to thin now, and he saw her coming. He parried one blow, then another. It was only on the third that her saber slipped through the man's defenses, cutting him down smoothly. By then, men were already closing in, and Kate had to run again just to burst through the circle of hands that grabbed at her.

There were too many of them. She was fast, and she could fight, but there were men closing in on all sides now, and even she could fall under the weight of numbers. She cut one down, but more were closing, and she was running out of room to run. She took a chance, reaching out for the strange, unfathomable power she'd touched once more.

As suddenly as it had come, the mist lifted.

Kate found herself staring at Lord Cranston's men, drawn up in order, with their weapons raised. For the second time in less than a minute, Kate threw herself flat as fire roared over her head into the enemy's ranks. Then Lord Cranston's men were charging, and the battle swept over her, into the ranks of the now depleted enemy forces.

A hand clasped Kate's, pulling her up. Lord Cranston was there, standing in the middle of the battle while around him men fought and died. And ran. The enemy were running now, making for their boats with the terror of men who knew they had little chance of making it.

"As your commander," he said, with a stern look, "I really must reprimand you for going off alone, without any orders. It was a foolish, idiotic thing to do."

Kate stood there, not knowing what to make of that, at least until Lord Cranston smiled.

"But I'm glad you did it," he said. "You saved us, Kate. The men won't forget that, and neither will I."

"Kate! Kate! Kate!" the men around her yelled as they lifted their weapons into the air.

Around Kate, the battle was winding down, and she could see some of the men looking at her with something like awe. It seemed as though, in a matter of minutes, she'd gone from merely Lord Cranston's servant to the hero of the battle. More than one came up, clasping her hand as if she'd just done something impossible. Kate saw Will over by one of the cannons, waving. She wanted to go to him, but there was no way to leave Lord Cranston's side with his eyes on her.

There were other eyes watching her too. Kate saw the crow sitting on the edge of the battlefield, staring at her with an intensity that had nothing to do with anything natural. It watched her for a moment or two longer, then took off in a flurry of movement.

Kate knew that it wasn't over. They'd won the battle, but something had just noticed her presence.

And that could only mean more danger.

CHAPTER TWENTY FOUR

Sebastian stood impatiently outside the doors to his mother's chambers, waiting for the moment when he would be allowed inside. Even he had to wait, because as his mother had often told him, she didn't have the luxury of ever being anything less than the Dowager.

Sebastian sometimes wished that he could be something other than a prince, though. It would have made things simpler with Sophia, for one thing.

He could hardly believe, as he stood there, that she had done all that Angelica had said about her. That she had come here in a fury looking for him, and ended up hurting Rupert. He hadn't wanted to think it was real, but it was what the guards were saying too: that they'd chased her after she'd attacked the prince.

Sebastian swallowed at that thought, thinking of what might have happened if they'd caught her. He was glad that they hadn't, even if she had struck Rupert. He knew his brother, and it was hard to believe that Rupert might not have done something to deserve it.

The harder part was that she had come there to tell him how much she hated him. That part was impossible to get past. A part of Sebastian wanted to believe that it couldn't be true, but everyone in the palace had seen Sophia there. They'd seen her running out, after everything that had happened. He knew that she had to hate him.

He deserved her hate, after what he'd done in sending her away. He deserved the pain of his wounds, because they weren't even close to being enough punishment for not having the courage to ask her to stay. When he'd met Sophia's sister, he'd assumed that she would try to kill him, and the truth was that if she had, it would have been no more than he deserved.

There was no time to think about that now, though, because servants chose that moment to come from his mother's room, throwing the doors open for him to enter.

"Prince Sebastian," one announced, as if his mother hadn't been the one to send for him in the first place. It was a ruler that he was there to see, his queen rather than just his mother.

"Come in, Sebastian," his mother called, and there was an informality to it that was at odds with the rest of it. She was there in the sitting area of her suite of rooms, perched informally on the edge of a chaise with a set of tea things laid out on a small table in front of her. Sebastian had no doubt that it would be the finest the Far Colonies had to offer.

She rose to meet him, forestalling his attempt to bow by wrapping her arms around him. It was one of the few times Sebastian could remember his mother hugging him like that. Normally before, there had been servants or courtiers, others to do the jobs involved in raising him, while simultaneously seeming to preclude closeness with their very presence.

"I'm glad that you're safe," his mother said, holding him in the hug for a moment longer. "When I heard everything that the messengers had to say… I didn't want to believe it. I told them that if they were lying to me about my son being in danger, I'd have them sent away in disgrace."

Sebastian could imagine her doing that, but it didn't make him feel better. Even in what he suspected was a declaration of motherly love, there was still a reminder that the formality of the court could never entirely go away.

Sebastian hated it. Normally, he could cope with the falseness and the shallowness of it all, the need to do not just the right thing but the expected thing. Yet it had been all of that which had meant he hadn't felt able to marry Sophia. It had been all of that which had forced him to put her aside, leaving her hating him. Any reminder of it, right then, was too much.

"Sebastian, are you all right?" his mother asked, reaching out to touch his face. Sebastian realized that she was examining the cut on his cheek. "Do your wounds hurt much?"

"A little," Sebastian admitted, although right then he wanted the pain, because it seemed to match the rest of him. What Sophia obviously felt for him had torn his heart in two. What was a little physical pain compared to that?

"I shall send for the finest physikers," his mother assured him. "They will stitch this wound, and it will look like nothing more than a handsome dueling scar. It will be dashing."

"Dashing?" Sebastian echoed. He could hear how flat his voice was, the pain he felt inside stripping the emotion out of it. "Was that how you wanted me to look when you sent me on an expedition to slaughter farmers, Mother?"

His mother stood back, looking stern for a moment.

"Those farmers had declared themselves in opposition to the crown," she pointed out. "They were traitors."

Sebastian thought of pointing out that the days when the king or queen had been able to arbitrarily decide that were long gone.

"You think I shouldn't have sent you?" his mother asked. "They were clearly an enemy of the crown. Fighting them was a chance to show the people around you that you are a strong prince, of use to the realm."

"By the people around me, you mean the Assembly of Nobles?" Sebastian demanded. "After what happened in the civil wars, you think they'll be impressed by a prince who goes around slaughtering his mother's subjects?"

His mother fixed him with a level gaze that had very little to do with the warmth or concern she'd shown before.

"People respect strength, Sebastian. Kindness, generosity, and all the other fine qualities that you have are only of use if you have the strength to *do* something with them. As a ruler, I can do more good than any dozen others in my realm, but it is only possible if I have the strength to hold my position."

"You speak as if these farmers could have overthrown you," Sebastian said.

His mother stood in silence for a moment or two.

"Alone? No, of course not," she said. "If it didn't matter either way, I might even let them have their scrub-covered little island. But it does matter, because if others were to hear that they succeeded in their uprising, what then? There are already occasional assassins, and idiots who sing their songs against the monarchy. A good quarter of the nobles in the Assembly were on the wrong side in the wars, or had fathers who were, at least. You think they wouldn't fight it all again if they thought they could win?"

Sebastian didn't have any answers to that. He didn't remember the civil wars, although he'd heard the stories about them, the same as everyone else. He'd seen the lasting tensions sometimes, expressed in old grudges and pointed comments.

"And so you sent me to have an easy fight against farmers," Sebastian said. "Just as you sent Rupert into easy battles."

"You think I should truly risk my sons?" his mother shot back. "Who would do that?"

Most of her subjects' mothers got no choice in it. Even so, Sebastian let it go, because he could understand the need to keep someone safe. What would he have done if Sophia had been in danger? Besides, the truth was that he'd found far more on the Strait Islands than farmers.

"It was the New Army there," he said.

"So your messenger said," his mother replied. She moved to the chaise, sitting and gesturing for Sebastian to do the same. She poured tea as if Sebastian hadn't said anything. Like that, she could have been the image of an older noble widow in a kind of semi-retirement, with little to do beyond planning the next ball or touring her estates. Yet this wasn't some lesser noble. This was his mother, the Dowager.

"What do you intend to do about it?" Sebastian asked.

"I have already given instructions to deal with the immediate threat," his mother said. "As for whatever might follow... we will deal with that as it becomes necessary. We are not without fighting men. The free companies, for all that they claim impartiality, are unlikely to stand by and allow their homes to be destroyed."

It seemed like a gamble to Sebastian, relying on mercenaries. More than that, it felt like an attempt to make him stay home safely again, when the last thing he wanted then was safety. He didn't deserve it. If Sophia hated him, he definitely didn't want it.

"Send the royal cavalry," he said. "Let us hold the line. I've fought the New Army before, and succeeded."

"Winning one battle doesn't mean that you have to win all of them," his mother countered. "This realm has many soldiers, but very few princes. I do not have enough sons to start risking them."

"Rupert is the heir," Sebastian insisted. "And you still allowed him his place in the army. If I fight the invaders, it will look good. You said yourself that people respect strength."

He said it, although the truth was that he didn't care about any of it. It was just what he had to say in order to be thrown in the direction of the conflict. If Sophia hated him, then Sebastian wanted to lose himself in that violence and be swept away by it. If he'd known how much she hated him when he was back on the Strait Islands, perhaps he would even have stood still on that beach and let the next musket ball claim him.

Or perhaps not. Sebastian didn't want to live without Sophia, but he wouldn't waste his life either. No, he would throw himself into the hardest parts of the battle. He would fight the enemy with everything he had, and would simply have to hope that somewhere out there, there was someone with the strength or skill or luck to end the sheer emptiness that welled up inside him at the thought of all he'd lost.

"I don't want to lose you," his mother said. "Sebastian, I know that things didn't turn out well for you with the girl you brought to see me, but that is no reason to throw yourself into the heart of a war."

It felt like the best reason there was, from where Sebastian was standing. It wasn't a surprise that his mother had noticed that Sophia was gone, because after all, the servants and the guards reported to her. He had to wonder, though, what she would think if she knew all of it.

"Mother," he said, "my mind is made up. I have my commission with the royal cavalry, and I will do my part in any conflict to come."

"You will do as you are told," his mother said. "Remember that it is a *royal* regiment. It will go where I command, and if you think that it will be anywhere near true danger, then you clearly aren't listening, Sebastian."

"Why, Mother?" he demanded, standing. "What does it matter?"

She rose, taking his hand in hers. "It matters because you are my son and I love you. Besides, I have more important matters for you than mere battles."

Sebastian couldn't think of anything more important right then. None of it seemed to mean anything, so what could his mother have in mind that was more important than an invasion?

"What are you planning, Mother?" he asked.

"When you announced your plan to marry that girl, I was happy for you," his mother said. Sebastian noted that she didn't use Sophia's name. "And when the arrangement fell through, I could see how upset you were. I want to do something that will make you happy."

Sebastian stood there in silence, because he had a horrible feeling that he knew what his mother was about to say next.

"I was pleased by the engagement, because the truth is that it is time you were married, Sebastian. It seems clear that Rupert won't be settling down just yet, and so it falls to you, as a matter of duty. Of honor."

"I can't marry," Sebastian said. "Sophia is gone."

He saw his mother shake her head in obvious exasperation. "You say that as if she is the only girl in the world who might be a suitable match. She isn't. Far from it, which is why I have taken the time to arrange a suitable match for you myself."

Sebastian stared at her in disbelief. "What?"

He supposed he should probably have guessed at it. It wasn't as though young men of his rank typically had the luxury of settling their own marriages, when such things could contain so many nuances of diplomacy and succession, alliance and dowry. He just hadn't expected his mother to see the gap left by Sophia's absence and decide that it needed to be filled like a child receiving a new puppy to replace a lost one.

"Mother, this isn't—" Sebastian began, but his mother was talking again.

"I have arranged a match," she said. "And a far more suitable one at that, although don't worry, the girl in question is quite lovely. I have spoken to her parents, and the engagement is set except for the formality of the Assembly's approval. You even know the girl, which I'm sure will smooth things somewhat."

"Who?" Sebastian asked, although even as he asked it, the possibilities started to take shape in his mind.

"Why, Milady d'Angelica, of course," his mother said. "I am sure that she will be perfect for you. She will certainly be perfect for the kingdom."

Sebastian stood there in silence. Finally, he did the only thing he could think of to do: he turned on his heel and walked out, leaving his mother staring in his wake.

CHAPTER TWENTY FIVE

Sebastian stood in his rooms, throwing things into a travel bag and trying to decide what was important. Money would be useful. Spare clothes for the journey, but not the finery of the court. Sebastian looked around. How much of this really mattered? Maybe if he'd realized that earlier, it wouldn't have come to this in the first place.

He could feel the pressure of time ticking away as he packed. Every moment was one in which his mother might decide to keep him in the palace by force, invoking her authority as his mother, his queen, the commander of his regiment. Probably the only reasons she hadn't done it already were that she didn't really think that it was possible that he might leave, and she was worried about the scandal that might come from a prince being hurt trying to get out of his own palace.

He was going, though, because he had to. If he didn't, then there was no chance that he would ever find Sophia. No chance that he could ever make this right.

"Maybe there is no chance," Sebastian said, but he hoped that it wasn't true. He knew he didn't deserve Sophia. Her sister had made that abundantly clear, even if Sebastian hadn't known for himself the harm he'd caused. He'd pushed Sophia away, putting his duty ahead of what he felt for her. He'd thrown her out onto the street, where she'd been taken as little more than a slave, whatever the kingdom's laws said about the nobility of indenture. He'd told her that he couldn't love her, when that was anything but true.

He didn't deserve to be able to make this better, but he had to find a way. If that meant leaving Ashton and traveling blindly until he found some news of her, he would. Sebastian would do whatever it took to get her back.

"Sebastian? What are you doing?"

Sebastian turned to find Angelica entering his rooms. Now that he knew about the marriage arrangement, he could see the simplicity of her dress, the gentleness of her manner, for what it was: no more than an attempt to snare him by being something he could find acceptable.

"What does it look as though I'm doing, Angelica?" he demanded. "I'm packing to leave."

He saw her frown at that. She did it prettily, of course, but her beauty had never been the point. He should have known that there was more to her helping him with his wound than simple kindness.

"Leave?" she said. "Surely they're not sending you away to fight again before the wedding?"

"So you knew about it, then," Sebastian said. He wasn't surprised. It was just confirmation of everything he'd been thinking since his mother announced this.

"About the wedding?" Angelica said. "Yes. Your mother told me about the arrangement she'd made with my father. I didn't tell you because... well, I thought she would want to tell you something like that herself, and because I thought it might be good to get to at least know a little of the real you."

It all sounded so plausible, but around the court, plausibility was common currency. Sebastian wasn't sure *what* to believe right then.

"So you didn't find a way to make this marriage happen?" Sebastian asked. "You didn't push my mother into it?"

"How could I?" Angelica asked, and the demure look she gave him might have been more believable if he hadn't seen her looking exactly like that at a dozen parties. "Do you really think that *I* have enough power to make the Dowager do anything she doesn't want to do?"

She had a point with that, and Sebastian calmed just a touch. Not even Angelica could force this marriage. It was his mother's doing.

"Your mother summoned me to her," Angelica said. "She told me that she had arranged the marriage with my parents, and that the matter was settled. Yes, I told her that I was happy with the prospect, but I didn't set it up or have any choice in it."

"And that doesn't make you angry?" Sebastian asked. His own anger was bubbling below the surface: at what his mother had done, at the situation he faced, and at his own stupidity in pushing Sophia away. If he hadn't done that, things might be different. They might have been getting married even now.

"Why should it?" Angelica asked, spreading her hands. "Do you think I haven't known my whole life that my entire worth comes down to finding a match to a suitable lord? That I would probably have no say in it anyway? With you, I know I am marrying a kind, gentle, handsome man. A prince, no less. Does it matter so much that I don't have a choice? I know you will make me happy."

Sebastian wasn't so sure about that. He'd managed to destroy Sophia's happiness thoroughly enough.

"I can make you happy too," Angelica said, stepping forward to drape her arms around Sebastian's neck. "I promise."

She kissed him then, and it was a different kind of kiss from the ones he'd had with Sophia. There was skill behind this, and control. It was a good kiss, but it was good because it was a well-practiced thing, not because of any connection between them.

"That wasn't so bad, was it?" Angelica asked. "I know you must think all kinds of things of me, Sebastian, but you will have time to get to know the real me once we're married. Now," she said, pulling him toward the bedroom, "I know you have your wound to consider, but we'll find a way to work around it. I'll help you to forget all about your objections."

Sebastian pushed her back then, and it was probably harder than he intended, because she stumbled.

"No, Angelica. No. I don't want to forget Sophia. How can you think that I would? You think that I can just jump into a marriage and hope to be happy?"

"What choice do we have?" Angelica countered. "Shouldn't we at least try to make the best of it?"

"We both have a choice," Sebastian said. He wished he'd realized that a long time ago. "I'm making mine. I'm sorry, Angelica, it's not that you've done something wrong, but it's Sophia I want. I'm going after her, whatever my mother says. I'm going to find her, and I'm going to persuade her to forgive me. She's everything I need. The *only* thing I need."

Put like that, he probably didn't need to spend any more time packing. He walked for the door, grabbing his few possessions on the way. So long as he found Sophia, the rest of it didn't matter.

***

Angelica very deliberately picked an expensive vase to break first. A second-era jewel glaze, by the look of it, which had probably taken the finest craftsmen days to produce a hundred years ago. It broke into fragments with a satisfying crack.

Sebastian wasn't there to hear it, of course. Angelica wasn't about to let him see this, because that would be evidence of the pain that he could cause her, and she wasn't in the business of allowing people to see that. In any case, the kind of woman to whom he was attracted was demure and delicate, not given to fits of carefully judged rage.

Because she wasn't done with it, she broke a mirror next, not caring about the glittering slivers that scattered across the floor. A servant would pick them up soon enough.

How had this happened? That question nagged at the edge of Angelica's thoughts. How had Sebastian rejected her? The idea of it had seemed so impossible before that she hadn't even considered it. She had assumed that the dutiful prince would have married his horse if his mother commanded it, and she was a long way from that.

She was refined, she was beautiful, she was educated. She had very carefully cultivated every accomplishment that a young woman should have, from languages to music, good taste to dancing. She brought with her a connection to one of the kingdom's old families, and at least a moderate fortune. If Angelica hadn't just broken the nearest mirror, she might have surveyed herself in it and seen the perfect example of nobility, constructed with all the care of a fine house or a beautiful bauble. Any man should have been falling over himself for her hand.

Yet Sebastian had rejected her. He had turned and walked out as if she hadn't even been there.

That was unthinkable. Angelica had made a special effort for him, noting his dislike of gaudy clothes, trying to show a more human side to herself, even kissing him with all the skill and passion that came from hours of practice in quiet corners of noble gatherings. He should have been begging her to marry him, yet instead, he had gone off on some fool's errand.

All because of Sophia, the girl who definitely wasn't from Meinhalt, who wasn't the kind of noble she should be, who had gotten in Angelica's way from the first moment she arrived.

Angelica couldn't see what it was Sebastian saw in her. She had nothing, *was* nothing. Angelica could probably find a dozen girls as beautiful anywhere in Ashton she looked. She had no accomplishments. The fact that Sebastian was going after her was even more of an insult because of that.

It was more than an insult—it was dangerous.

Angelica could still remember kneeling on the floor of the Dowager's rooms, listening to the old hag talking about the mask of lead as if it were nothing. Angelica didn't know if she would make good on the threat, but she could remember the fear she'd felt at the time, the certainty that her life was about to end in the most horrific way possible.

She'd said that she would do anything, and the Dowager had given her what had seemed like a simple enough task at the time: making sure that her son forgot all about Sophia. The Dowager would not be happy to learn that Angelica had failed to even keep Sebastian in the building.

Angelica sat on one of the chairs in Sebastian's rooms, trying to decide what she could do next. She didn't panic. She *refused* to panic, because panicking was what silly, lesser girls did when faced with problems. Screaming and fainting had their place, but only as weapons to attract sympathy or attention, not as anything to be done when there was no one else around. Now was the time for sitting quietly, considering the implications, and then acting.

Should she run? The idea of it seemed ludicrous, yet if she was about to incur the Dowager's wrath, maybe it was the only option available to her. If Angelica could make it out into the country, far enough ahead of any pursuers… no, that wouldn't work. There was nowhere that the Dowager's influence couldn't reach within her kingdom, even if some parts were usually outside her attention.

Abroad, then? Angelica could take what she needed and leave, going across the Knifewater or out to one of the colonies, near or far. The difficulty with *that* was that there would be nothing waiting for her. Her father had business interests abroad, but Angelica would effectively be starting with nothing. She had no wish to do that.

That left effectively one option: she had to kill Sophia.

The thought sat in her mind as coolly as a stone, and Angelica was a little surprised by how calmly she considered it. She had done other, lesser things in the past, of course. She had drugged rivals and embarrassed them, used secrets to control others and bought debts simply so that she could destroy those she needed to. Murder, though… until now, it had always seemed like some line that could never be crossed.

But what alternative was there? She could find another way to get rid of the girl, but then Sebastian would probably keep searching after her. She could hope that he didn't find her, but that might take years. No, Angelica needed something decisive. Something that couldn't be traced to her, of course, but something final, after which Sebastian might run to her in his grief.

Angelica stood, a little surprised with herself. If she'd known that plotting murder would be this straightforward, perhaps she would have done it years ago.

She just needed to find Sophia before Sebastian did.

CHAPTER TWENTY SIX

They pressed on quickly after the inn, with Sophia glancing behind them every so often to make sure no one would follow once they'd found their bravery at the bottom of a beer flagon.

There was no sign of anybody following, though. Maybe they'd decided that the young man at the inn had deserved everything that had happened to him. More likely, Sophia guessed, they simply didn't want to risk the trouble. She had no illusions about what kind of world this was. In her experience, people cared a lot less about justice than they did about their own safety.

What did it say, that this was such a cruel place? Sophia couldn't help wondering if it was the result of the wars, or the kind of example the royal court set, or something else. Maybe the whole world was like this, and people everywhere sought to take advantage of those weaker than them. Sophia hoped not, but she wasn't sure that her hopes could change things for anyone. Her hopes hadn't been able to make things work with Sebastian, or secure her a place at Ashton's court.

Perhaps they could lead her to her parents' home, though, and provide some answers to the things that still lived on in her dreams. She had more memories than Kate of the things that had happened when they were children, but it had still taken Laurette van Klet to tell her who her parents even were.

"How much further do you think it is?" Cora asked, as the cart continued to roll along roads that had obviously been washed out at some point and then only haphazardly replaced.

That was hard to say, because Sophia didn't know exactly where it was they were going. It seemed that they'd gone through more landscape than could ever exist, and she knew that Cora felt the same way after the city. Only Emeline seemed at ease with it all, seeming to enjoy the wide spaces and the freedom they offered.

"It can't be too much further," Sophia said. "The last people we asked said that we couldn't be more than a day from Monthys."

"We still have to find the estate once we get there," Emeline pointed out, although she seemed happy enough about the prospect of it. Sophia knew how eager she was to get there so that they could go and look for Stonehome.

"We will," Sophia said. She tried to sound more confident than she felt. Even though they'd already come all this way, it still felt a little unreal, as if it were impossible to risk dreaming that they might actually find the spot they sought.

Then the cart rolled up to the crest of a hill, and Sophia saw it.

At least, she saw *something*. It was still away in the distance, worked sandstone standing out against the sky as the afternoon sun caught it. There were hills all around, and forests that seemed to stretch out like a carpet in between sloping fields more suited to grazing sheep than anything.

Was it a great house, an old castle, or something else? At this distance, it was impossible to make out any real details of it, and yet Sophia felt herself drawn to stare at it there, feeling a connection to it even though she couldn't say exactly what, or why.

"There," Cora said. "It's actually there."

Even Emeline seemed pleasantly surprised by the sight of it. "We actually did it."

Sophia wanted to nod, but she'd already seen what lay between the hill they were on and the road that led into the trees, toward the estate. The ground seemed to break apart like a wound there, a gorge splitting the greenery with a stretch of gaping darkness.

"Perhaps we can go around," Emeline said, but the gorge seemed to be so long that it would take them a day out of their way in any direction to do it, even if they could find a way through the rough landscape.

A slender white line across the gorge seemed to offer a sliver of hope.

"There," Sophia said, "a bridge. If we hurry, we can make it across before darkness falls."

Sophia urged the horses toward it, the cart moving forward as they pulled. The road was smooth here, and they made swift progress down toward the spot where the bridge sat. Sophia was grateful for that. She wanted to make it to her parents' lands before they stopped for the night, even if she doubted that they could go all the way to the stone structure she'd seen in one go.

As they got closer to the bridge, Sophia started to get more of a sense of the scale of it. It was huge, crafted in white marble, wide enough that two carts could have fit on it side by side. That was just as well, because there were spots where the stone seemed to be crumbling from lack of attention, with holes in the surface that would take every inch of the available space to steer around.

They rolled out onto it with Sophia steering, Emeline and Cora jumping down to both lighten the load and allow them to spot crumbling sections of stonework. There were plenty of those, and Sophia found herself holding her breath as she crossed.

The whole thing looked so ancient that it might have been built before the kingdom came into being. Certainly before the Dowager's ancestors rose to the throne. Most of it seemed to fit together seamlessly, and now Sophia started to see the spots where cannon had done what time couldn't, taking chunks out of the bridge in the course of some forgotten battle. Sophia felt one of the cart's wheels start to fall into one of the holes, and she urged the horses to the left, hoping that she had reacted quickly enough. Here on the bridge, she doubted that she and the others would be able to pull it out.

The horses complained at the effort, but with a squeal of wood, the wheel popped clear. Sophia was more careful about the line she chose across the bridge then, the cart moving forward at barely more than a walking pace.

By the time they reached the other side, the light was starting to fade, and Sophia felt more tired than she'd thought she might, after the concentration required on the bridge. Somehow, she didn't feel as worried about the possibility of people following them here, either. The bridge felt like a boundary as much as a connection. As much as she wanted to get to her parents' home, as much as she wanted to see it up close, she knew that wasn't going to happen tonight.

"We should camp here," she said.

***

They made camp on the edge of the trees, in a space near the road but sheltered from the sight of it so that they could set a fire. They were all too exhausted to hunt, so they ate trail rations and drank the little beer that hadn't had them hiding in it. Sophia tossed Sienne scraps of meat and the forest cat seemed more than happy with them.

Her stomach seemed less happy with it all, roiling at the taste of the food and making her gag. Sophia rose with difficulty, stumbling toward the edge of their campsite, because she didn't want to throw up in front of the others.

"Are you all right?" Cora asked.

Sophia managed to nod. "I'll be fine," she said. "I'm just—"

She had to stop speaking as another wave of nausea threatened to overwhelm her. Was there something wrong with the meat? She all but ran for the edge of the trees, managing to make it beyond their camp by a matter of strides before her stomach betrayed her and she crouched in the bushes, losing everything she'd eaten.

"Are you sure you're okay?" Emeline asked.

"I'm fine," Sophia said. "It must be something I've eaten."

Except that they'd all eaten the same things, and there was no sign of Cora or Emeline becoming sick. Sophia didn't feel unwell either, except for the nausea and everything that went with it. If she were ill, wouldn't she have felt something in the last few days? Wouldn't there have been some build-up to this rather than this sudden and overwhelming sickness that felt like…

…no, it couldn't be, could it?

Sophia stood there, trying to remember what she could of the methods wise women used for these things. The girls at the orphanage had chattered about such things as if they were worldly and knowledgeable, while the nuns had sometimes scared them with the certainty that they would know if they stepped beyond the bounds that had been set.

There were herbs that reacted to the urine of pregnant women differently, weren't there? Mother's Sign and Clarrisent, although Sophia only knew what the first one looked like, having seen the small, feathery flowers once.

She looked around for it, not even knowing for sure if it grew in woodlands. If she had any sense, she would call out for the others and ask for their help. She would send a message to Kate, and ask for her assistance in locating the herbs. She didn't do either one, both because it felt as though she'd spent most of her life recently begging for others' help and because she wanted to know for sure before she even thought about saying something.

There was another reason too: this was hers. She didn't want to have to share this moment.

She kept searching, working her way through the nettles and the wildflowers, the moth-attracting mosses and the broad leaves of the trees. Finally, she saw something that looked as though it might be the right flower, although even then, how could she be sure?

Right then, Sophia wished that she knew more. She wished that she had parents who could help her with it, or that she really was the noblewoman she'd pretended to be, surrounded by servants who might know what they were doing. She would even have settled for the knowledge of one of the nuns, and that was a more than desperate thought.

She knew then that she needed the help of the others, but she hitched up her skirts first, standing over the herbs while she did what was necessary.

"Cora, Emeline, help me please." Sophia tried to make herself sound calm. She didn't want to sound as though she was being attacked by bandits, or dying from some ague brought on by the food.

Even so, they came running, hurrying through the trees as if they were certain that something awful had happened to Sophia. Perhaps it had, or something wonderful, or both. She wasn't entirely certain what she felt in that moment, staring down at the leaves of the Mother's Sign as they wilted in the way she'd been told they would.

The two of them stared at her, obviously trying to work out what was going on. Sophia could even feel Emeline pushing at the edges of her thoughts, although Sophia didn't let her penetrate any deeper than that. She didn't say anything for several seconds, continuing to look at the herb as if that might somehow change the result.

"What is it?" Cora asked. "When you ran off, you didn't look at all well."

"Did something happen?" Emeline added. "Is it the people from the inn?"

Sophia shook her head. "No, no, it's nothing like that."

For the moment at least, she had forgotten all about the people who had tried to rob them, and all the other dangers of the road. Those didn't matter, compared to this.

"What is it then?" Emeline asked.

Sophia took a breath. She wasn't even sure that she could say it, because it was just too big.

"I think…" she managed, "that I'm pregnant."

CHAPTER TWENTY SEVEN

Kate hadn't thought that she would be able to see the blacksmith's shop again, let alone rumble toward it with a cart filled with the swords and muskets of the enemies she'd defeated. That was what she was doing, though, because Lord Cranston had sent her with them for re-forging and for the steel to be used in armor plates. He'd also given her a pouch of coins: her share for fighting with the company. Kate had never been paid for working before. She'd always been indentured to be commanded, or an apprenticed there to learn.

Will had his own small pouch of coins. He rode on the wagon with her, looking happy at the bonus, and at having come through the battle unscathed. Kate could see enough of his thoughts to know that wasn't the only reason for his excitement. He was happy about going home, but also happy about being there with her. She sensed it every time he looked her way, staring at her as if he was seeing her for the first time.

Kate liked those looks, and wished that there were time for more than looks. Perhaps there would be, later.

For now, they rumbled through the outskirts of Ashton, to the spot where Thomas's blacksmith's shop sat. The smith must have seen them coming, because he was outside, and so was Winifred. Kate wasn't surprised to see that they were smiling, because their son was coming home safely, but she was surprised that they both seemed happy that she was coming to them as well.

"Will, Kate, you're back!" Thomas said. Will leapt down and Kate waited while the smith and his wife swept up their son in a crushing hug. She was a little surprised when the three of them pulled her down to join them, folding her into a family embrace that she'd never experienced before.

For practically the first time anywhere, she felt as though she belonged. She handed over the coins she'd earned to Thomas, knowing that he could use them more, and she could see Will doing the same. It seemed his parents wouldn't be short of money anytime soon.

"Come inside, both of you," Winifred said. "There's stew warming over the fire. I know Thomas will want you to help him

163

melt down all those swords, but you're not doing it without some food inside of you."

Kate didn't argue with that. She hadn't eaten anything since the battle, because the sight of it had driven all appetite from her. Now, though, hunger came to her in a wave. Winifred showed her inside, and fussed over her while they ate. The transformation from the woman who had been so suspicious of her before was remarkable.

As for Thomas, he seemed eager to hear all about what had happened.

"You were fighting against an invading army?" he asked. "Not just raiders?"

"An expeditionary force," Kate said, trying to downplay it a little. She could see how worried Thomas was about them. He knew what soldiers went through, and if she started talking about the New Army or the Master of Crows, she suspected that would make it worse. "We managed to fight them off."

"*Kate* fought them off," Will said. "The rest of us were pretty much spectators."

He sounded a little in awe of everything she'd done. Frankly, even Kate had been surprised that she was able to do it; however, she didn't want to sound as though she was the hero of it all.

"I didn't do everything," she said. She reached out for Will's arm. "I'm pretty sure that I saw plenty of cannon fire going on."

She wasn't just trying to make Will feel better, but to be fair, that was a big part of it. The rest of the company had played their part in the battle, and she wasn't going to claim all of the credit in front of his parents.

"Well," Winifred said. "I'm just glad that the two of you are back in one piece. I couldn't stand it if something happened to you." She looked over to Kate. "Either of you."

Kate was a little surprised by how much that meant to her.

They ate slowly, and as with her time in the forge, Kate found herself thinking about how wonderful it would be to have this forever. It was simple, peaceful, and quiet in a way that so much else in her life wasn't. Would this be how things would have been if she hadn't gone to the forest to learn to fight? If she hadn't gone back to the House of the Unclaimed for her revenge?

Winifred and Thomas didn't ask her about that part of things. She could see from their thoughts that the watchmen had visited them to find out where she was, but neither of them seemed to have the horror that Kate might have expected from people who had heard about what she'd done. Maybe they understood what the orphanage did, too.

164

"We should probably start to move the steel into the forge," Thomas said eventually. "If I start to get the forge up to temperature, can the two of you sort through it all to find the pieces that can be salvaged and the ones that are there to melt?"

Kate nodded, and Will practically jumped up to help.

They worked together, sorting through the salvaged weapons and armor, picking out the obviously broken ones first, then trying to assess the dented pieces to see which could be salvaged and which would forever be weakened by the damage.

"Thanks for telling them I played a part in the battle," Will said with a smile.

"You did," Kate assured him, reaching out to squeeze his hand. That contact sent a thrill through her, the simple touch seeming like far more than that. "Do you think I would have gone down there and fought all of them without you and everyone else there to back me up?"

"You seemed to do a pretty good job alone when the mist came," Will said. He paused for a moment. "I was terrified for you when I saw what you were doing. I thought I was going to lose you."

"Ah, so you have me?" Kate asked.

"No, that isn't what I… I meant that…"

Kate grinned at that. "It's okay, Will. I was worried for you too. I wanted you to be safe, and… yes, I didn't want to lose you."

She moved closer to him, her hands resting gently on his arms. From there, it just seemed natural to lean up and kiss him. She hadn't kissed him since she'd gone to the free company. She'd barely had any time alone with him, when Lord Cranston's disapproval of any romantic distraction was so obvious.

Now, though, Kate wanted to be distracted. She wanted to hold to Will and remind herself that there was more to life than violence, killing, and revenge. She wanted to remember that there was love too, even if that did make her sound more like her sister.

"We could wander off," she suggested. "Find somewhere quiet?"

She wanted to do that almost more than anything. She wanted to make the most of the time she had with Will, and not waste a moment of it. She wanted to kiss him then, and not stop kissing him.

"How is that steel coming?" Thomas's voice from the forge reminded her that the rest of the world was still out there, and there were things that they needed to do in it.

Perhaps he'd seen them and decided to interrupt as politely as he could. Perhaps the forge was simply getting close to the temperature he wanted it. Either way, the effect was the same. Will and Kate pulled back from one another, and Kate caught Will's slightly sheepish expression.

"We should probably finish this," he said.

Kate nodded, reluctantly. "But later…"

"Later," Will agreed.

Later had the same kind of sound to it Kate might once have associated with a magical land or a dream. She sat on the edge of the wagon while Will took in the ruined steel, ostensibly checking for further faults, but actually just thinking about Will and what might happen with him. Those thoughts were delicious, drifting into daydreams.

Kate felt the moment when daydreams shifted over into visions, the familiar images of ochre-clad foes appearing. They were still stalking through Ashton's streets, the House of the Unclaimed burning in the background. Kate didn't know if it was a combination of elements that had already passed now, or a warning about the future, or something else.

She walked the streets, and now the streets of Ashton opened onto locations that had never been there. The beach was somehow off one of the alleys there, wreathed in mist, with the dead shambling out of it. Burning corridors that she remembered from her childhood stood in place of winding streets. Somehow, a giant sundial stood in place of the palace, the shadow it cast moving around slowly, people dying wherever that darkness touched them.

Kate shook her head, and she was back at the forge, sitting on the edge of the wagon. She hopped off, hoping that walking would clear her head. She walked around the side of the forge, trying to get some fresh air in its small garden.

She was startled to find Siobhan there, standing in the middle of it.

Siobhan smiled in a long silence.

"Things are progressing faster than I anticipated," Siobhan said.

"What things?" Kate asked. "I'm supposed to be your apprentice, but you haven't told me half of what's happening."

Siobhan took a step back, into a patch of earth. Vines sprang up and seemed to flow over her in rivulets.

Siobhan stared at her for a long time, too long, her eyes piercing through her.

Finally, she grinned. An evil grin.

"It's time," she said.

It was all she said, and yet her words pierced Kate's heart like a dagger. Those two words, she knew, would change the course of her life forever.

It was time, she knew.

It was time for Siobhan to ask her favor.

A SONG FOR ORPHANS
(A Throne for Sisters—Book Three)

"Morgan Rice's imagination is limitless. In another series that promises to be as entertaining as the previous ones, A THRONE OF SISTERS presents us with the tale of two sisters (Sophia and Kate), orphans, fighting to survive in a cruel and demanding world of an orphanage. An instant success. I can hardly wait to put my hands on the second and third books!"
--Books and Movie Reviews (Roberto Mattos)

From #1 Bestseller Morgan Rice comes an unforgettable new fantasy series.

In A SONG FOR ORPHANS (A Throne for Sisters—Book Three), Sophia, 17, journeys in search of her parents. Her quest takes her to foreign and strange lands—and to a shocking secret she could never imagine.

Kate, 15, is summoned by the witch, as her time has come to repay the favor. But Kate is changing, coming of age, become ever more powerful—and what will become of Kate if she makes a deal with darkness?

Sebastian, a romantic, follows his heart, throwing it all away to reject his family and find Sophia. But Lady D'Angelica is still bent on killing her—and may have other plans.

A SONG FOR ORPHANS (A Throne for Sisters—Book Three) is the third book in a dazzling new fantasy series rife with love, heartbreak, tragedy, action, adventure, magic, swords, sorcery, dragons, fate and heart-pounding suspense. A page turner, it is filled with characters that will make you fall in love, and a world you will never forget.

Book #4 in the series will be released soon.

"[A THRONE FOR SISTERS is a] powerful opener to a series [that] will produce a combination of feisty protagonists and challenging circumstances to thoroughly involve not just young

adults, but adult fantasy fans who seek epic stories fueled by powerful friendships and adversaries."
--Midwest Book Review (Diane Donovan)

Books by Morgan Rice

THE WAY OF STEEL
ONLY THE WORTHY (Book #1)

A THRONE FOR SISTERS
A THRONE FOR SISTERS (Book #1)
A COURT FOR THIEVES (Book #2)
A SONG FOR ORPHANS (Book #3)

OF CROWNS AND GLORY
SLAVE, WARRIOR, QUEEN (Book #1)
ROGUE, PRISONER, PRINCESS (Book #2)
KNIGHT, HEIR, PRINCE (Book #3)
REBEL, PAWN, KING (Book #4)
SOLDIER, BROTHER, SORCERER (Book #5)
HERO, TRAITOR, DAUGHTER (Book #6)
RULER, RIVAL, EXILE (Book #7)
VICTOR, VANQUISHED, SON (Book #8)

KINGS AND SORCERERS
RISE OF THE DRAGONS (Book #1)
RISE OF THE VALIANT (Book #2)
THE WEIGHT OF HONOR (Book #3)
A FORGE OF VALOR (Book #4)
A REALM OF SHADOWS (Book #5)
NIGHT OF THE BOLD (Book #6)

THE SORCERER'S RING
A QUEST OF HEROES (Book #1)
A MARCH OF KINGS (Book #2)
A FATE OF DRAGONS (Book #3)
A CRY OF HONOR (Book #4)
A VOW OF GLORY (Book #5)
A CHARGE OF VALOR (Book #6)
A RITE OF SWORDS (Book #7)
A GRANT OF ARMS (Book #8)
A SKY OF SPELLS (Book #9)
A SEA OF SHIELDS (Book #10)
A REIGN OF STEEL (Book #11)
A LAND OF FIRE (Book #12)
A RULE OF QUEENS (Book #13)

About Morgan Rice

Morgan Rice is the #1 bestselling and USA Today bestselling author of the epic fantasy series THE SORCERER'S RING, comprising seventeen books; of the #1 bestselling series THE VAMPIRE JOURNALS, comprising twelve books; of the #1 bestselling series THE SURVIVAL TRILOGY, a post-apocalyptic thriller comprising three books; of the epic fantasy series KINGS AND SORCERERS, comprising six books; of the epic fantasy series OF CROWNS AND GLORY, comprising 8 books; and of the new epic fantasy series A THRONE FOR SISTERS. Morgan's books are available in audio and print editions, and translations are available in over 25 languages.

Morgan loves to hear from you, so please feel free to visit www.morganricebooks.com to join the email list, receive a free book, receive free giveaways, download the free app, get the latest exclusive news, connect on Facebook and Twitter, and stay in touch!

68160624R00100

Made in the USA
San Bernardino, CA
30 January 2018